"西安外国语大学学术著作出版基金"资助出版

西安外国语大学文丛

纳博科夫

之

"他者"意识空间构建

郑 燕◎著

中国社会科学出版社

图书在版编目(CIP)数据

纳博科夫之"他者"意识空间构建:英文 / 郑燕著 . —北京:中国社会科学出版社,2015.5

ISBN 978 - 7 - 5161 - 6103 - 6

Ⅰ. ①纳… Ⅱ. ①郑… Ⅲ. ①纳博科夫,V. (1899～1977) - 小说研究 - 英文 Ⅳ. ①I512.074

中国版本图书馆 CIP 数据核字(2015)第 095004 号

出 版 人	赵剑英
责任编辑	任　明
责任校对	林福国
责任印制	何　艳

出　　版	中国社会科学出版社
社　　址	北京鼓楼西大街甲 158 号
邮　　编	100720
网　　址	http://www.csspw.cn
发 行 部	010 - 84083685
门 市 部	010 - 84029450
经　　销	新华书店及其他书店

印刷装订	北京市兴怀印刷厂
版　　次	2015 年 5 月第 1 版
印　　次	2015 年 5 月第 1 次印刷

开　　本	710×1000　1/16
印　　张	11
插　　页	2
字　　数	186 千字
定　　价	55.00 元

凡购买中国社会科学出版社图书,如有质量问题请与本社营销中心联系调换
电话:010 - 84083683

Acknowledgements

The time when I first read Nabokov is when my mentor——Professor Jun Liu (Tomming), a professor of English department in California State University introduced me to Nabokov's *Lolita* several years ago. I remembered that once I started reading it, I was enchanted by Nabokov's sensuous and keenly observed fictional world that is not without the shadows of his own life of exile. And at the same time I was deeply puzzled by the intentions of Nabokov in writing such a complicated yet "playful" novel as *Lolita*. I have an instinct that Nabokov has more concerns that go far beyond the generally discussed and accepted themes and forms among the critics. Being curious, I started to read Nabokov's short stories and his other fictions and I know that the themes and concepts that concern Nabokov are also something that I want to know why and how they are composed. Urged by this motive, I decided to take Nabokov's books as my project for my Ph. D dissertation and extended my study on both literary criticism and contemporary theories in hope of deepening my understanding on Nabokov after graduation. During this process, it is Professor Tomming, an expert on both European literature and Nabokovian works who provides me with his considerations on issues important relating to Nabokov and modern literary studies at large, guiding me onto a track that is a cultural reading of the modernity of Nabokov's books in Nabokovian sense of the world and literature.

I would also like to extend my greatest gratitude to my Ph. D. Supervisor/ spiritual mentor——Professor Shi Zhikang. His complete trust in me, his philosophy of happiness in both life and art, his enthusiasm and passion in reading the texts themselves, all encourage me to concentrate on the mission of the writing of my book. The "otherworldly" bliss that I am rewarded by the writing of Nabokov's texts strongly coincides with Professor Shi's preaching of the aesthetic pleasure that he obtains from his own creation and imagination in his literary realm and his elegant world of language. In addition, Professor Shi's active and affirmative reconstruction of happiness also echoes Nabokov's will to happiness. Guided by my professor's passion of art, I am ready to start my conscious journey toward that pleasure of the otherworld. Besides my supervisor, I also obtained great help and encouragement from my other professors. The detailed and insightful interpretations of literary works conducted by Professor Li Weiping, the well-read Professor Yu Jianhua, the theoretical Professor Zhang Dingquan all made great impact on me and will further set examples in my future literary studies and researches.

I also want to show my gratitude to Rugang Li, my husband, whose understanding and support enable me to concentrate in my reading and writing while talking off my pressure when I am stalked by some tricky problems in the writing of some parts of my book. My Mum and Dad, Huamin Zheng and Zhihong Cai, offer me great help in listening to my complaints, relieving me of pressure by their thumb knowledge and taking care of themselves for all these days of my writing. I also thank my parents-in-law——Yongsen Li and Xuying Wu for the great foods that they had prepared for me during my painstaking work.

Finally, I want to give my gratitude to my colleagues in XISU: Jiang Yajun, Dang Zhengsheng, Yang Dafu, Li Xiaoou, Wang Jing for their phone calls, messages, and get-togethers to liberate me from the intense work. Special thanks should also go to Yang Xiaoming who kindly provided books from USA and The School of English Studies of XISU for purchasing books about Nabokov for me from USA. I also give my special thanks to the librarians——Mr. Shi and Mrs Lu in Shang Hai International Studies University for their great support in providing first-class service to me to support my writing.

This book is to my daughter——Letong Li.

Yan Zheng

August 23, 2014

Montreal, Canada

Preface

This book gives special consideration to Vladimir Nabokov's sensitivities to the past, the self, and the otherworldly truth. With these perspectives and nexus combined together as starting points, the book intends to deliver the idea that Nabokov is reinscribing a speaking "self" in his three representative English works of his mature period of creation from 1935 to1950—*Invitation to a Beheading* (1935), *The Real Life of Sebastian Knight* (1941), and *Speak, Memory: An Autobiography Revisited* (1966) (first finished in 1950 under the name of *Conclusive Evidence*). This speaking self is an "I" pinned in an in-between space between the mundane world and the otherworld, between the fictional and the realistic, between personal history and public history and is seen through the other or the otherness that is both part of an externalized "I" and part of a repressed "I" . The self refers to the writer self and the other refers to the self's outwarded insideness, an outward projection of the inner "I" . This other or the otherness of the self is Nabokov's literary ruse of self-expression. By projecting the innermost feelings and ideas onto the other——a doubling of a past "I", an aesthetic "I", and a cultural "I", Nabokov tends to reach his self through those fictional others and others' others/doublings, making experiments and playing with the concept of "I" artistically and magically in philosophical, psychological and cultural spheres so as to utter a speaking "I" .

As a literary strategy, the self is metaphysically expressed through the self's double in *Invitation to a Beheading*, through the self's outward projection in a character/narrator/writer (Sebastian) in a literary world of metafiction— *The Real Life of Sebastian Knight* and through Nabokov's combination of cultural self of his Russian past and his present diasporic self (since no "self" that is confined in prison of time and space can fully express an ever-changing identity of a cultural self as Nabokov's) in *Speak, Memory*. This writer self is disguised respectively in the character self as Cincinnatus and his doubling in *Invitation to a Beheading*. It is hidden in V. and his half-brother Sebastian Knight in *The Real Life of Sebastian Knight*. And it can be again found in the fictional/past "I" and the historical/present "I" in *Speak, Memory*. The otherness of the self has a strong sense of the existence of the otherworld and is seen forever striving for something else that is not to be found here and now, but there—a timeless, blissful realm free from confinement.

Put in the context of an imaginative otherworld, my concept of self which contains both the character self and writer self merges from time to time with each other and it is difficult to tell the real one from the imaginative one. As for the two roles played by the self—a character self and a writer self, they are combined to be Nabokov's self-conscious literary device of deception so as to artistically express his own speaking "I" in its doubling/other. Therefore, in this sense, "I" is the other. This character self, i. e. the other of the writer self, is seen yearning for the otherworld in these three selected works in different ways. And it is this very other that can fully show its idiosyncratic infiniteness, difference, and tolerance when being located in this longed-for otherworld context. Therefore, the otherworld ideal leads them to the ultimate state of delight, providing them with an imaginative space to escape from the prison of the vulgar. In these three works, this speaking self, when is projected in Nabokov's works as characters, takes the form of both a character "I" and a writer "I" partly because the three selves in the three books all act as both a character and a writer in the book and partly because they all carry strong consciousness of Nabokov.

The self in *Invitation to a Beheading* is seen as a character, imprisoned in the cell, striving for a truer realization of his self partly through being a letter writer to disclose the secret he embraces—the "secret" of the otherworld. We can see there is always a double which is opposite to or complementary with him. When the character self is striving to be a writer "I", inscribing his understanding of his half-brother in verbal expressions as we find in *The Real Life of Sebastian Knight*, this writer "I" is constructing his identity in a more self-conscious way so as to explore the ecstasy of the otherworld that art pursues. When this "I" is the character/writer, moving between fiction and autobiography, between art and history as a diasporic writer in autobiography *Speak, Memory*, the self now takes the form of a cultural hybridity, a reinvented self with difference and otherness in it. Therefore, this newly-invented self starts to take an otherness with it, ceasing to be the former, national self. When the otherness is planted into "I", the "I" is a new self with inventions and a new life. It ceaselessly travels, transforms among and disperses different cultural elements in the new context of international culture. As a result, a very creative "I" is formed.

On the other hand, the otherness in the self is also reflected in the lost "I" in the past. This "I" in its primacy returns ceaselessly to the present context, influencing and making impact on the present self for its utterance. From the perspective of Lacanian psychoanalysis, the signifiers of the other are making efforts to take the place of the lost "I" in imagery stage. Therefore, a series of signifiers tend to refer to the lost "I", only to show that these signifiers are the signifiers of the other. Nabokov, through a detour to the other and the otherworld, actually expresses the well-disguised "I" and the Russian literature and culture that he has hence individually transformed. This is exactly the essence of Nabokov's art. In my analysis, I will employ both structural and thematic approaches to illustrate my point with more attention given to the theme. And the analysis of stylistics and structures is conducted to support my interpretation of the theme of Nabokov's texts. I will prove that Nabokov, in his works discussed here, consciously reinscribes his own speaking self through his unique literary ruses and tactics such as doubling (the outwardness of the insideness of the self), self-*in*-other and self-*is*-other to express his metaphysical, literary and cultural positions in the much-desired otherworld textual space that he has all the way constructed.

It is exactly in this seriously constructed otherworld space that Nabokov's works are twice detached from the down-to-earth verisimilitude in art so that his art, in the fictionality of fiction, is exceptionally ambiguous, open and fictionally imaginative. And his speaking "I", amid the details of the mundane world, is humane, poignant and willing in a positive way for the possibility of happiness obtained through conscious seeking for the otherworld. It is also through his otherworld sensibility that we readers can detect the true intentions of a writer as unique as Nabokov: in the otherworld space where he can break the time barriers of the mundane world, Nabokov achieves an unusual power of looking at this world from the other side of the boundary between life and death. Through this keen perceiving power and the aesthetic bliss obtained, his innermost self is seen, expressed and constructed in an artistic way of imagination.

Nabokov's appropriations of his characters so as to utter in a concealed way his own anxiety both as a writer and a man and his obsession and creative recombination of his personal past with his present self are signs to prove that he is writing himself, the selfest of his own self through metaphysical thinkings, literary experiments as well as through conscious construction of his cultural position. In examining the relationships between the self and the other (the externalized self, the otherness of the self, the difference within), the private and the public, the past and the present, the mundane and the otherworld, this speaking subject— "I", taking disguises fictional or authorial in different works, matures and evolves by creating an independent and individualistic self in the context of the mundane and the otherworld in *Invitation to a Beheading*, by gaining literary independence through writing a biography of a fictional double in the context of literary artifice in *The Real Life of Sebastian Knight* and by writing an autobiography, connecting a personal history with the impersonal art, that is, a historical "I" transformed and reinscribed in the fictional context of the repressed memories returned in *Speak, Memory*.

My innovative ways of interpretation of Nabokov's three works selected here are as follows: 1) the writer of the book introduces the narrative strategies of Nabokov to the interpretation of *Invitation to a Beheading* and *The Real Life of Sebastian Knight* for a more substantial approach. And this approach does not exist for its own sake. It is always led to clarify the theme that this book concerns. 2) the writer of the book creatively adopts a cultural perspective to interpret the speaking "I" in *Speak, Memory* for contextual perspective. By extending from the aesthetic analysis to a cultural interpretation of the work, the writer of the book attempts to better address the writer's unspeakable and unutterable intentions. 3) the writer of the book holds that in his way of reaching the other-world ideal, Nabokov consciously reconstructed an aesthetic context of his remote Russian past, only to express in a more unique and artistic way his own self, only in a hidden way. This result of my research in Nabokov's literary works from another angle proves Nabokov's exact illustration of his own critical ideas in his discursive writings. 4) Through the analysis of the cross-over boundaries of the self (both writer self and character self), the writer of the book meant to say that the self is expressed through nothing than the other, both in literary and cultural senses. 5) Through the theories of Freud's " the uncanny" —the return of the past, Lacan's linguistic signifiers of the other, Michel de Certeau's the other in the discourses and Homi Bhabha's play of Freud's unhemlich in cultural context, the writer of the book tends to expand the understanding of Nabokov's art into its cultural dimension so as to create a substantial reading of his art while paying attention to his claim of aesthetic bliss.

The body part of the book is divided into three sections and they respectively focus on the metaphysical, the literary and the cultural aspects so as to see in a clearer way the expression, development and transcendence of the speaking "I". The first chapter deals with the self's trans-crossing between the mundane and the otherworld in *Invitation to a Beheading*. Through various stages of growth of consciousness, the self in this book finally gains his independence and power in combating with the mundane and enters his otherworld awareness. By figuring out a structural patterning in the construction of both the mundane world and otherworld on the part of Nabokov, I attempt to prove that the speaking "I" in the fiction is composing his own metaphysical identity within as against the without.

The second chapter sees the self-conscious construction of a self's gaining gradually an intellectual and artistic independence in the process of composing another man's biography in *The Real Life of Sebastian Life*. This speaking "I" crosses over the boundary of the reality and fictionality, merging the dividing line of the two worlds of facts and fiction. In this process, the speaker finally realizes that the real life of his biographee—Sebastian is the fiction, i. e. the book itself. Therefore, inscribed in the text is the speaking "I", who, after many obstacles in the very process of gathering the writing materials for his biography, finds his true artistic identity, hence accomplishing the hard-earned literary independence.

The third chapter is mainly on the authorial self since the book *Speak, Memory* discussed in this chapter is claimed to be an autobiographical novel which is unusually more fictional than many other autobiographies. The speaking self in it is a Nabokov who constructs a cultural self in the "beyond", traveling spiritually in-between home and abroad while creating his self as a cultural hybridity. Writing in a more conscious way of the former unconsciously-accepted home culture, the speaking "I", as a result of distancing from the home culture in time and space, can gain for itself more perspectives in an international context of culture, thus seeing itself in a more objective, detached way. And to no exception, all the selves in the three chapters are seen to strive for a timeless and ecstatic otherworld which Nabokov seeks in both his life and art.

List of Abbreviations

CE	*Conclusive Evidence: A Memoir*, New York: Harper, 1951.
G	*The Gift*, Middlesex: Penguin, 1983.
IB	*Invitation to a Beheading*, Middlesex: Penguin, 1983.
LL	*Lectures on Literature*, New York: Harcourt Brace Jovanovich, 1980.
LRL	*Lectures on Russian Literature*, ed. Fredson Bowers, New York: Harcourt Brace Jovanovich/Bruccoli, 1981.
Mary	*Mary*, Penguin Book, 1971.
NG	*Nikolai Gogol*, New York: New Directions, 1961.
RLSK	*The Real Life of Sebastian Knight*, Norfolk, Conn: New Directions, 1941.
SL	*Selected Letters*, Harcourt Brace Jovanovich, 1968.
Stories	*The Stories of Vladimir Nabokov*, Middlesex: Penguin, 1995.
SM	*Speak, Memory*, New York: G. P. Putnam's Sons, 1966.
SO	*Strong Opinions*, New York: McGraw-Hill, 1973.

Contents

Introduction

As a Russian émigré writer writing in both Russian and English languages, Vladimir Nabokov summarizes his own life in his autobiography-cum-fiction *Speak, Memory* (1966) as "a colored spiral in a small ball of glass" and sees his life as three stages of repetition with new surprising turns in each phase of life:

> The twenty years I spent in my native Russia (1899—1919) take care of the thetic arc. Twenty-one years of voluntary exile in England, Germany and France (1919—1940) supply the obvious antithesis. The period spent in my adopted country (1940—1960) forms a synthesis—and a new thesis. (*SM* 275)

Leaving Russia from the year 1919 for European continent when the October Revolution in 1919 destroyed the Tsar's reign, Nabokov, born in a noble aristocratic family and whose father is a democratic liberal (neither supports Tsar nor has faith in the red army of the revolution) was forced to exile along with his family. They first went to Crimea that is located at the south part of Russia and then to Berlin and never came back to the motherland for their whole lives. Taking a journey forever away from home and being a writer with all his tentacles open to respond to the rich and multi-national political, social and cultural currents, Nabokov makes full use of this experience and creates from its very essence (distilled from his memory of the past) the most humane and original representation of a speaking "I" in adapting the self to the outside world by way of a self-conscious awakening that is leading him forever toward the other-world.

Nabokov's fiction is renowned for its intricate allusiveness, linguistic play, and elaborate authorial patterning. Scholars such as W. W. Rowe explores the spectral signs and signals solely to evacuate meanings concerning the function of ghosts and sexual implications hidden in Nabokov's works. However, Nabokov's works do not stop at that. His works, with rich plays of signs, meanings and patterns, aim to express particular themes, longings and desires that are hidden amidst those seemingly unconnected elements and nexus. Studies conducted by Brian Boyd are insightful in that he incorporates Nabokov's style with his themes so as to dig out structural patterns that govern the seemingly unrelated details and patterns that are wrought around the growth of the consciousness on the part of the protagonists in Nabokov's major later works such as *Pale Fire* and *Ada*. Another scholar Julian W. Connolly in her *Nabokov's Early Fiction: Patterns of Self and Other* conducted studies on Nabokov's works through an approach of the combination of both theme and style. She points out that there is an evolving growth in the relationship between self and other. She divides Nabokov's early Russian novels from 1924—1939 into four stages in terms of this relationship of self and other, with a concern also given to Nabokov's narrative strategies.

Here, this self and other are different from Julian Connolly's self and other. Her self and other respectively refer to the character self and writer self as fixed entities. My self and other refers to the writer self and the otherness of this writer self that is projected out as this self's double. In this sense, the two selves cease to be any fixed stereotypes, but they become flowing and changeable substances, repeating, splitting and merging with each other in any creative way possible. For me, this writer self is disguised as the characters——Cincinnatus and his doubling in *Invitation to a Beheading*. In *The Real Life of Sebastian Knight*, it lies in characters—V. and his half-brother Sebastian Knight. And in *Speak, Memory*, it is found in the fictional / past "I" and the historical / present "I". The otherness of the self has a strong sense of the existence of the otherworld and is seen forever striving for something else, not here and not now, but there—a timeless otherworld realm free from any confinement. Put in the context of an imaginative otherworld, my concept of self which contains both the character self and writer self merges from time to time with each other and it is difficult to tell the real one from the imaginative one. As for the two roles played by the self——a character self and a writer self, they are combined to be seen as Nabokov's self-conscious literary device of deception so as to artistically express his own speaking "I" in its doubling/other. Therefore, in this sense, "I" is the other.

This character self, i. e. the other of the writer self is seen yearning for the otherworld in these three selected works in different ways. And it is this very other that can fully show its idiosyncratic infiniteness, difference, and tolerance when being located in this longed-for otherworld context. Therefore, the otherworld ideal leads them to the ultimate state of delight, providing them with an imaginative space to escape from the prison of the vulgar. In these three works, this speaking self, when is projected in Nabokov's works as characters, takes the form of both a character "I" and a writer "I" partly because the three selves in the three books all act as both a character and a writer in the book and partly because they all carry strong consciousness of Nabokov.

Out of Nabokov's more than a dozen major fictions and sixty-five short stories, the three books that I have chosen for the present study are written in his middle and late period (1935—1950). *Invitation to a Beheading* was finished in 1935 and *The Real Life of Sebastian Knight* was finished in 1938 and published in 1941. As we know, the late 30's was the time when Nabokov developed his otherworld sensibility and has matured as a famous writer and translator in Berlin Russian émigré circle. After 1940, he went to America and about ten years later he finished the best autobiography ever written—*Speak, Memory* (1966) (earlier it is revised and called *Conclusive Evidence*, finished in 1950). These three novels see Nabokov test the construction of a self striving for independence, creativity, individuality in confronting with the mundane world while striving for the otherworld. The sui generis construction of a unique individual is achieved respectively in these three novels: 1) the self is buried deep in the mundane and finally is awakened at the moment of death for a self-constructed otherworld in *Invitation to a Beheading.* 2) the self in *The Real Life of Sebastian Knight* strives to write a real true biography of his half-brother's life history and is enlightened finally at the end of the book, discovering that his very narrative—the fictional book itself is the truest real life of his half-brother, thus transcending reality into fictional otherworld. 3) the self transcends time and space, past and present, private and public history so as to break the boundaries between these categories to retrieve the past self in the present, a repressed self that returns to speak for itself in a diasporic writer's life and art. With the discussion of each of the three novels, we can see more clearly that Nabokov is showing greater self-consciousness in reconstructing a speaking "I" in all three sides: the metaphys-ical, the literary, and the cultural.

In addition to these three major works, Nabokov's certain short stories that were composed during the period of time—from 1935 to1950 will also be briefly discussed since Nabokov's treatment of thematic material in the shorter works of-ten anticipates his handling of similar material in the longer works and the longer works are in a way the extended form of the short ones. When each of the novel and short stories are discussed, the theme, along with the structure of a given work, is equally examined because either one of these studying approaches is insufficient in discussing fully Nabokov's works, the former being too flexible and deprived Nabokov of his uniqueness in appropriating the conventional motifs and the latter too narrow-minded and deprived Nabokov of his metaphysical depth. In addition, since Nabokov's speaking "I" is not merely a self confined passively within the aesthetics but also a cultural self standing in the forefront where various cultural forces meet and fight, Freud, Michel de Certeau and Homi Bhabha's ideas will be introduced to help probe into Nabokov's self in his adapting to his émigré status.

Although these three philosophers are unrelated at first sight, the latter two incorporated Freud's idea of uncanny in their own works. According to Freud, the uncanny is "that class of the terrifying which leads back to something long known to us, once very familiar" (Freud 123). By going back to the origin of the German version of English word "uncanny", Freud scrupulously traces the word *unheimlich* (literally unhomely) which means "the name for everything that ought to have remained ⋯ hidden and secret and has become visible" (Freud 129). Then the unfamiliar and strange are actually familiar things and have been known for a long time and that it has become strange is because it has been repressed. When the repressed returns, it can cause an uncanny feeling, a feeling similar to horror and weirdness. When it comes to literature, the unhomely is always presented in the theme of a "double", that looks alike with another in this or that way, doubling, dividing and interchanging between these two splitting selves.

Later, Michel de Certeau in one section of his *Heterologies: Discourse on the Other* discusses de-constructively that, in Freud's scientific works and Freud's idea of the return of the repressed, there exists an otherness of literary discourse hidden in Freud's scientific discourses. This otherness is the repressed, giving no regard to the logical scientific studies of Freud. It bites and upsets the superficially rational discourse of psychological science of Freud. According to Certeau, the psychoanalysis's (as against the historiographist's) way of distributing the space of memory is to recognize the past in the present, treating the relation as one of an imbrication (one in the place of another), a repetition (one produces the other in another form). Though the past is repressed,

It resurfaces, it troubles, it turns the present's feeling of being 'at home' into an illusion. It lurks—this 'wild,' this 'obscene,' this 'filth,' …within the wall of residence, and behind the back of the owner (the ego) or over its objections, it inscribes the law of the other. (Certeau 2)

From this sense, like what Certeau says about Freud, Nabokov's art of memory is the repressed returned. The past is repressed by the present narrative but it speaks through silence from the gap of the present composition.

Homi Bhabha also makes use of the idea of "unhomely" in his *Locations of Culture*. In it, he claims that the diasporic writers, in the condition of extra-territorial and cross-cultural initiations, reveal the unsaid and the unspoken that should have been hidden. This has caused the ambivalence of the boundary between the private and the public spheres on the part of the writer. In this case of these diasporic writers, he remarks "this results in redrawing the domestic space as the space of the normalizing, pastoralizing, and individuating techniques of modern power and police: the personal-*is*-the political, the world-*in*-

the-home" (Bhabha 1338). Viewed from this perspective, Nabokov's works, when being read and reread, do reveal hidden webs of meaning that are well beyond the superficial.

The richness that has been introduced into the formerly simply set symmetries of the nations and worlds makes the already fixed categories of home and world uncertain. Under the disguise of art, Nabokov asserts his cultural position as a diasporic writer who reinscribes his self in the intricate invasions of history and voices his homeliness in an unhomely context through the re-cognization and re-presentation of the home in a new way when one is distanced from it in time and space. When the recognization of home culture is reached, the presencing of this very moment makes the already taken-for-granted home culture stand out as something new in the perspective of a marginalized and displaced émigré as Nabokov. The reconstruction of the self in the bridge of home and world—the "beyond" where the homeliness and unhomeliness meet demonstrates the past returned in a strange way.

In addition to his expansion of Freudian idea of the unhomeliness, Bhabha holds that people in exile always ingeniously and creatively experience social differences as a vision and construction— "that takes you 'beyond' yourself in order to return, in a spirit of revision and reconstruction, to the political conditions of the present" (Bhabha 1333). This "beyond" in Bhabha's sense is an in-between space that the diasporas invent to insert and reinscribe their identity. Maneuvering in this liminal space, Nabokov summarizes his personal life history in his autobiography *Speak, Memory* as a spiral in an impersonal art, a spiral as an open space that "has ceased to be vicious··· [and] it has been set free" (*SM* 275). This spiral metaphor is both literally and figuratively precise in that it is a space that twirls around time but it incorporates forever larger circle or arc of other elements (the otherness) in every moment of upward twirling. With forever increased space of each of the arc at each new stage, the spiral space of Nabokov contains the repeated memories as well as his innovative re-appropriations of these "traditions" . Therefore, through re-appropriation and accommodation, Nabokov retrieves his past in an inventive way so as to enforce his own order and meaning in an uncontrollable situation thrown at him by fate. The self-created space of spiral with its strong self-consciousness coincides in a way with Nabokov's idea that "there are three kinds of beings in the world: "time without consciousness—lower animal world; time with consciousness—man; consciousness without time—some still higher state" (*SO* 30). Staying in the second high, Nabokov's art is seeking all the time for that highest timeless level of consciousness—otherworld, where the prison that formerly confines man's consciousness in the mundane world is completely destroyed.

To examine Nabokov's art in the way that Nabokov himself understands his art, one has to consider the all-pervasive otherworldliness in Nabokov's works so as to see what Nabokov really aims at in mapping out tensions in the characters, images and events for a true meaning of existence. Nabokov's widow Vera announced in her "Foreword" to the posthumous collection of Nabokov's Russian poems published in 1979 that "*potustoronnost*" is Nabokov's main theme and stresses that, although it "saturates everything he wrote" (Alexandrov, *Nabokov's Otherworld* 5), it does not appear to be noted by anyone. The Russian word "*potustoronnost*" that Vera used is a noun derived from an adjective, denoting a quality or state that pertains to the "other side" of the boundary separating life and death. This word is translated into English as "the hereafter", "the beyond" . But it is Vladimir Alexandrov's translation into the "otherworld" that arouses the least disagreement. Although Nabokov never utters this word both in his fictions and non-fictions, he did keep portraying this metaphysical world of artistic creation starting from the mid-1930's, not only in the genre of the short story, but also in novels, poetry, drama and even his early attempts at memoirs in the 1920's.

Then what does this "Otherworld" really mean? Is it a religious term or a term tinged with some romantic notion of quest and idealization of the things unattainable in the mundane world, eulogized by poets and writers in many cultures? In "The Art of Literature and Commonsense" which was published posthumously in 1980, Nabokov, in expressing his sui generis faith in a transcendent realm, pronounces his idea of an unutterable, mysterious state of immortality by making a contrast with the idea of commonsense:

That human life is but the first installment of the serial soul and that one's individual secret is not lost in the process of earthly dissolution, becomes something more than an optimistic conjecture, and even more than a matter of religious faith, when we remember that only commonsense rules immortality out. (*LL* 377)

By saying that "human life is but the first installment of the serial soul," Nabokov seems to give priority to the other side of the boundary of life and death than this side when he is speaking of the issue related with the soul. By saying that "one's individual secret becomes more than an optimistic conjecture," Nabokov exorcizes the romantic conventions or cliché of personal quest for an ideal object or vehement yearning for a departure for some paradise where love and beauty reign eternally though he does not exclude them in his otherworld since he says the secret is *beyond* that simple "optimistic conjecture. " Thus, Nabokov's otherworld is within but at the same time beyond the literary aesthetics. It is something both aesthetic and metaphysical. By saying that it is "even more than a matter of religious faith, when we remember that only commonsense rules immortality out," Nabokov transcends the religious faith of the existence of a paradise and extends it to artistic and individual creativity that rule out the bland and unimaginative institutional hypothesis of the generalities.

This "another dimension" (meaning the otherworld), though not clearly cited by Nabokov, is also in every sense, different from that paradise purely in religious sense. It can be a space in which the aesthetic bliss is achieved through artistic imagination. It might be a space transcending time and the trivialities in the mundane. It can be a space in-between this world and the otherworld, a space that Nabokov the artist creates solely as an artistic ruse to help him coping with an exile life. It might be a space from which another perspective is offered, a perspective that the man alive can never perceive. The otherworldly secret can only be perceived by the specially blessed characters created by the writer or by the characters bestowed with that epiphany that enables him to savor the wind blown from the other side of the door of life and death. The characters that are tinged with these sensibilities and consciousness of the writer are constructed as people in the mundane world of life, longing to obtain some otherworldliness or some truth from the otherworld through various means such as dreams, drunken state, obsession, insane state, heart attack or being on the verge of death.

Like what Shrayer says, Nabokov's otherworld is an antiworld which is related in terms of this world (23). By comparing the otherworld with this common-sense world in his "The Art of Literature and Commonsense", Nabokov parodies the mundane world, but at the same time, lucidly demonstrates that the mundane world in his works is a springboard from which the characters are uplifted to a higher world. If this is the case, then, aesthetically, the otherworld is where "the monster of grim commonsense" (*LL* 380) is shot dead and literary imagination begins to rule. Emotionally, "the otherworld is a domain of idealized timeless love, impossible in the mundane world" (Shrayer 23). In addition, there is some truth in Shrayer's remarks that there is not much to say about it other than saying it in Nabokov's own in terms of the otherworld (23). Though Shrayer does not say in a sure way what Nabokov's otherworld is, he does provide a way of looking at Nabokov's otherworld, that is, through Nabokov's own treatment of this timeless realm in relation with the mundane and its related side-product: the *poshlost* (untranslatable Russian term for a combination of self-satisfied mediocrity) that is radically criticized in Nabokov's works. He also emphasizes Nabokov's unique use of the otherworld by using Ellen Piffer's understandings of Nabokov's otherworld in character analysis: Nabokov's otherworld is "solicitous" (qtd. in Shayer 22), privileging his favorite characters with the gift of being able to see otherworldly beatitude and love.

All literary worlds strive to create a simulacrum of "real" space. This "real" space in quotation marks is, in Nabokov's sense, perceived through a subjective mind. That is to say, the "real" is the subjective perception of the objective world of reality. Full of details that the reader "should notice and fondle" (*LL* 1), this "real" world created by the artist is, in Nabokov's words, "invariably···a new world ··· When this new world has been closely studied, then and only then let us examine its links with other worlds, other branches of knowledge" (*LL* 1). Then this "new world" is what we say the mundane world or reality that has been processed and recreated by the author in an ingenious way in his literary works. Serving as an essential starting point for other worlds or other branches of knowledge to spring from, the mundane world is meticulously mapped out in Nabokov's art world. It is the material world that the characters can not live without but, at the same time, they strive to leave so as to perceive some truth about the otherworld. Further, for Nabokov, an original author always invents an original world. The readers therefore will experience the pleasurable shock of artistic truth if a character or an action fits into the pattern of that original world no matter how unlikely the person or thing may seem when they are transformed into the real world.

Nabokov the artist ingeniously cultivates the otherworld in such a way that it becomes something in his works as a battlefield where he utters his artistic individualities in contrast against anything that is labeled by him as convention, *poshlost* or vulgarity. At the same time, Nabokov the exiled Russian aristocrat makes the otherworld functional by storing in it his cherished memories of childhood Russia in which love and happiness reign. Nabokov's otherworld, along with the mundane world in his artistic works, combines to build a three-dimensional narrative space. The more accurate and exact Nabokov's world of art is represented verbally, the more control and defense he obtains for his world of art. This is because his maneuvering of his art world can offset in a large sense his uncontrollable living situation of exile. Therefore, by focusing on the otherworld and putting it in contrast against and paralleled with the mundane world, we can clearly see that Nabokov's art has both lucid thematic purpose and hidden structuring framework. From this perspective, Nabokov's world of art is a space uniquely and accurately designed to hold the treasures he cherishes all his life, decorated with creatures animate and objects impressed with memories of his childhood as well as his motherland Russia. It is also a platform on which something is determinably separated from conventions of both aesthetic and religious. In addition, it is an artistic realm in which one can find Nabokovian patterns of theme and structure disguised in various forms, thus allowing him freedom to create and construct his kingdom where he can control and maneuver, unlike the outside reality where he is marginalized. And all these owe to the pervasiveness of the otherworldliness in Nabokov's works.

Vladimir Alexandrov, in his *Nabokov's Otherworld*, gives a clearer definition of Nabokov's otherworld by basing on a hypothesis that Nabokov's works can only be appreciated by combining three perspectives—the metaphysical, the aesthetic and the ethic. By "metaphysical," he means that Nabokov's faith in a transcendent, non-material, timeless, and beneficent ordering and ordered realm of being that seems to provide for personal immortality, and that affects everything that exists in the mundane world. By "aesthetics," he refers to the theme of creation of art and the characteristic shape and style of his works. By "ethics," he means Nabokov's belief in the existence of good and evil and his belief of their accessibility as a universal criteria to the mankind, especially to the true artist who can guide and judge man's behavior. (5) Alexandrov believes that Nabokov's epiphanies of the "otherworld" are the sudden fusion of the trinity of the three and any one of the three can not be fully understood without the help of the other two. By devoting to these three aspects concerning otherworld, Alexandrov directs more attention to the relationship between the philosophy and artistic realization of that philosophy in Nabokov's life and art. Making these terms entangle with each other, his book in a way makes Nabokov's works appear to transfer much more profound philosophical ideas than that Nabokov aims at. It in a way complicates the issue and reduces the pleasure in appreciating Nabokov's art and otherworld sensibility.

The criticism conducted by Chinese Scholars on the theme of "otherworld" can only be seen in less than one third of the discussion done by Wang Xia's book entitled *The Cross-boundaries in Nabokov's Literary Works*. But she only sees the "otherworld" as one of the four parts of the cross-boundary phenomenon in Nabokov's works and does not discuss the "otherworld" by way of close-reading and deep exploration of the theme. (5) For the other published journal articles, most of them only take the "otherworld" as an aside or a way of talking to lead into various other analyses of themes. In addition, the criticism of Nabokov's works mainly concentrate on his major novels such as *Lolita*, *Pale Fire*, *Pnin* and *Ada*. For the less known ones, they are not analyzed in a full way and books such as *Speak, Memory* is mostly used to subsist the analysis of the other more popular ones. Among the criticism of both Chinese scholars and foreign scholars, the three novels are not discussed in depth in book-length except for Julian Connolly's book on *Invitation to a Beheading*.

Nabokov's works are permeated with a strong sense of otherworldliness. The difficulty of his art can only be more fully understood when it is discussed under the perspective of the otherworld. In *Speak, Memory*, Nabokov says:

> I confess I do not believe in time···And the highest enjoyment of time-lessness···is when I stand among rare butterflies and their food plants··· This is ecstasy, and behind the ecstasy is something else, which is hard to explain. It is like a momentary vacuum into which rushes all that I love. (*SM* 139)

This something else I believe is the truth which can only be reached in that timeless and joyful otherworld. In this otherworld space, Nabokov puts all his cherished things in it to experience the joy that frees him from the confinement of time as a prison. This space is the otherworld where death and pain are not to be found and happiness and love reign. But at the same time, Nabokov only knows too well that the otherworld is paradoxically established upon the mundane, the banality of which serves the very foundation from which the otherworld springs from. In delineating the mundane world in an exact way, Nabokov creates his ideas of the otherworld which would otherwise fail to be seen clearly solely on its own since it is so elusive and mystic in common people's eyes. It is in this context that Nabokov inscribes his self, speaking from the center of the texts to fulfill the spiral of his life along with the otherworld in his art.

Chapter One The Speaking "I" Pinned in the Mundane and the Otherworld in *Invitation to a Beheading*

Invitation to a Beheading, already the eighth Russian-written novel by the year of its completion in 1934 and publication in 1935, is said to be the "dreamiest and most poetical novel" by Nabokov in one of his interviews (*SO* 76). It is a story of a man called Cincinnatus C. who is sentenced to death for a crime called "gnotstical turpitude" (*IB* 61). This crime is described in the book indirectly as an "opacity", "occlusion" and "impenetratability" (*IB* 61). After reading the book, one could see that it is nothing more than his being different from all the other people who live without individuality and sense of perceiving the world in any subjective ways whatsoever. The book begins with the announcement of death sentence of Cincinnatus in the very first sentence. But no one knows when the beheading day will come, especially on the part of Cincinnatus. In the horrible process of waiting for the doom's day that may come at any time, Cincinnatus experienced many things that are out of his expectation.

In the huge fortress where he is the only prisoner, he has interviews with his family-in-law, his wife, his mother and has to deal with the jailer, the prison director, the executioner, the lawyer and the daughter of prison director. He is forced to make friends with the executioner—M'sieur Pierre in disguise of a newly-come prisoner who oddly strives to develop a friendship with him until Cincinnatus's execution day. During the 19 days of waiting, Cincinnatus expected that someone will come to rescue him and thought that he will be saved when he heard the insistent knocking at the wall. But it, along with his other expectations, turns out to be a complete trap and deception. With the biggest disappointment coming from his wife, Cincinnatus finally comes to realization that the better way of living is impossible to be found in this world, but rather in the otherworld. At the end of the story, Cincinnatus (figuratively) stood up from the executing block and walked firmly on his own toward "the voices that stood akin to him" (*IB* 191).

The novel starts with the culmination of the pressure of the trivial life forced upon Cincinnatus—the death sentence given by the society. And the novel ends with another culmination of spiritual rebirth—Cincinnatus's walking away from this world toward another direction, an otherworld where he finds things that are akin to him. This arrangement of the beginning and ending is significant because it highlights the existence of the mundane world and the otherworld as well as a character inserted in-between. The traveling from one world at the beginning of the book to the other at the end of the book incorporates a lot of elements for both Cincinnatus and his double to think and re-think: 1) What is most intolerable in the mundane world? 2) Can love be the final solution to the suffocating mundane world? 3) How does one cope with a world where people are automatons, feelingless and thoughtless, conforming to an unbearable second-class truth and self-satisfied mediocrity? 4) How can one see the otherworld truth in this mundane world? 5) Is death the final release of the spiritual otherworld from the physical body and the mundane? 6) How does one put the otherworld truth in words so that thoughts and expression can be united as one?

To answer these questions, Cincinnatus must undergo a series of setbacks in the mundane so as to prepare fully for entering the otherworld. When Cincinnatus first enters the cell, he starts writing something on the piece of paper. But due to the horror incurred from his death sentence, he can not smoothly express his ideas in logical and meaningful ways. He worries about his lack of time to write everything he wants to say to Marthe in the letter since the execution day will come any time. He is also full of fear of death itself though in the first sentence of the letter he said that he has the premonition of death. Fidgeting about the death coming at any moment, he has to deal with the director, the jailor and the lawyer in the prison. Almost every detail of the three's actions, conversations, ways of dressing are delineated scrupulously by the narrator as if Cincinnatus, along with the narrator, is witnessing or even watching these people coming and going, talking this way and that way while Cincinnatus remains in the darkness, hard to be approached and has little to respond or say to all these performances of the three. Pushed to the front and spotlighted as clowns, they serve as the essence of the mundane world from which Cincinnatus compares and as a result sees more clearly his difference from those people. His happy recollection of his love with the 15-year-old Marthe in his Tamara Garden, the bliss aroused by the pure air around that space that holds the things he cherishes so much are very much far beyond the wall of the cell. The more detailed the scenes and the prison staff in the cell are presented, the more metaphysical, profound, and enchanting the imagination of Cincinnatus becomes.

But before the day Cincinnatus is executed, he constructs his otherworld imagination around the wrong persons and things, attempting to inspire life from the lifeless. He cannot read some of the signs that actually denote the decay and cruelty in the people around him. He constructs his otherworld truth around a woman who starts to betray him by sleeping with other men from the first year of their marriage. Even so, he still dreams of forming a design "afterwards" (*IB* 51) that will suit both him and her, a unique design of love that no one in the earthly world will understand. When he reads the illustration drawn by Emmies, he believes that the little girl with a wild vitality of life and spirit hints at rescuing him. When Pierre is chatting with him, he is even on the verge of believing that he is the man who is knocking at the door and will come to rescue him. Though having flaws and weaknesses in figuring out the right way to the otherworld, Cincinnatus is firm in that he embraces the otherworld truth that no one in the mundane possesses. He sees the world in a more subjective, imaginative and associative ways by connecting and synthesizing different things to a unity or creating new feelings about the same thing. His heart impulses with the world outside and he tastes his otherworld bliss by deliberately setting his soul free such as in a dream, in closing his eyes to temporarily forget the body, in dividing himself into two selves. Through these ways of setting one's inner self free from both the physical body and the mundane world, Cincinnatus, with his shadow as a medium, can break the confinement of the mundane and enter his

Tamara Garden where he puts all his favorite things together to experience the timeless bliss.

Tamara Gardens contains his pleasant memories of the past with Marthe, the love and happiness that can never be retrieved in the present mundane. As a space that transcends time, excludes death and eternalizes love, Tamara Gardens transports Cincinnatus to a metaphysical level of the mundane world, the level in which the otherworld offers him another order, another insight, another perspective of looking at and perceiving the world. Cincinnatus and his double/ shadow that can go free out of his bodily confinement thus live another life, a life that can not be endured by the transparent people in the mundane. On the one hand, these common people isolate him, purge the shadow and the opaque out of him and try to reform him so as to assimilate him into another automaton that thinks and acts the way everybody else thinks and acts. Living among people of commonsense, Cincinnatus shapes and sharpens his consciousness and strives in a firmer way for the otherworld truth.

On the other hand, though otherworld truth is his life goal, the mundane world can not be totally cancelled out. There are several reasons for it: 1) The mundane world delimits a life with its details and trivialities. A life concrete and everyday provides a possibility, a need and a backdrop for a man like Cincinnatus to uplift his double to another state which is free of fixed rules, orders, reasons and laws of the mundane world. 2) It is the mundane and the vulgarities in this world that make Cincinnatus see more clearly his difference, his foreignness which would otherwise remain hidden. It is the transparent and "silent" mundane world (where people do not express anything individual, imaginative or subjective) that makes the voices that are instead akin to Cincinnatus stand out and be heard. Hence the new birth of a truly independent self. 3) Only when the details are specifically drawn about the mundane world can the metaphysical aspect stand out, be recognized, and then eagerly quested for by the self. Otherwise, being lack of substances, the otherworld will be nothing more than a mere fantasy. 4) Nabokov's otherworld is seen always full of many substantial things, events and people from the mundane. The difference between the substantial things in both worlds is that, in Nabokov's otherworld, the things and people selected from the mundane are infiltrated with humanity, morality, subjective perception, individuality, timelessness (achieved by breaking the boundary between the past, the present, and the future) and creativity/imagination. Being gilded with a shimmering tinged with memory, love, self-conscious construction, Nabokov's otherworld is a metaphysical world that is not vastly detached from the mundane, but connected with the mundane, only in a higher, metaphysical sense.

The self on the part of Cincinnatus, being pinned in this world and the otherworld, creates an in-between space that conforms to a rare time and in which he hides his inner self, his double. In this space, time is not physical clock-time, but subjective time created by Cincinnatus's double, his spiritual self who associates the unconnected things and people together to recreate a more lively and artistic meaning and relationship. Matured from the obstacles and depressions that torture him in the mundane world, Cincinnatus gradually possesses an independent consciousness. And in full awareness, he steps toward his otherworld upon execution, the inner self thus being released fully from the physical one. Besides moving towards the otherworld by splitting to his double, this dynamic self also seeks to verbal expressions to inscribe his identity and the otherworld secret he possesses. In the letter he wrote to Marthe, he shapes his ideas into expression and evolves from the writing possess a new self, voicing his views in a self-consciously constructed artistic world and assuming the characteristics of the otherworld in terms of eternity, creativity and imagination. On the one hand, like the author of the book, Cincinnatus the character and the writer steps into the otherworld through his writing. On the other hand, Nabokov, as a self-conscious writer, infiltrates himself onto the self of the protagonist, airing his suppressed voice through a detour of a tension between the mundane and the otherworld so as to create happiness in his artistic world. The core of Cincinnatus's otherworld is constructed around Tamara Gardens. The name of the garden can not fail for the readers of Nabokov to recall the name of Nabokov's adolescent sweetheart before he left Russian for good. Nabokov's love affair with Tamara is presented through a whole chapter of his autobiography *Speak, Memory* where he said "the loss of my country was equated for me with the loss of my love" (*SM* 245).

Is that Nabokov is self-consciously trying to regain his loss through artistic means by creating an "I" that speaks for himself? It is very probably so. If not, he is at least unconsciously doing so. Although he openly claimed that, as long as he lent some of his personal histories to his characters, these personal facts cease to have any relationship with him; his selection of these very details of his life history instead of others contains significant meaning. The name of Tamara Garden recalls his love lost in Russia. The otherworldliness around that name and that garden coincides with the otherworld constructed by Cincinnatus where he cherishes his lost Marthe, the Marthe at the age of 15, the Marthe in the past that can not be regained. But the inner connection between the two is further proved by the idea of the return of the repressed. According to Freud, the past simply refuses to go and it will lurk somewhere in one's life and emerge when chances occur. For Nabokov, Cincinnatus's disappointment at the mundane world is an artistic echo of Nabokov's dismay at what had befallen Russia. Haunted by the personal memory of his forever lost childhood in his homeland, Nabokov asked through Fyodor in his *The Gift*, his most nostalgic fiction that recalls his Russian life: "Ought one not to reject any longing for one's homeland, for any homeland besides that which is with me, within me⋯" (*G* 187)? This is precisely Cincinnatus's mission— "to reject his longing for a return to the homeland that has deceived him and to nurture instead his inner vision of a more perfect and fulfilling realm" (Connolly, *Nabokov's Invitation to a Beheading* 32). Against both the mundane life in Berlin and the disappointing homeland, Nabokov constructs an inner homeland that synthesizes both, but higher in a metaphysical sense in *Invitation to a Beheading*.

Ⅰ The Mundane World

The world that Cincinnatus lives in is a world that is "surrounded by some sort of wretched specters, not by people" (*IB* 31). These specters torment Cincinnatus as one is tormented by "senseless visions, bad dreams, dregs of delirium, the drivel of nightmares" (*IB* 31). This world, with the cell as its intense representation, is a "whole terrible, striped world; a world which seems not a bad example of amateur craftsmanship, but in reality calamity, horror, madness, error" (*IB* 78).

When we read *Invitation to a Beheading*, we will be intrigued to ask why in many scenes of the novel there are so many descriptions that hint at the theatricality. And this feature of theatricality is always linked with the characters who do not share the sensibilities of Cincinnatus. In chapter Ten when M'sieur Pierre comes to Cincinnatus' cell to coax him to act kind and nice and be a friend, the narrator makes this chit-chat scene a circus putting on performance, with Pierre as the circus joker and the prison director as the circus director, the cell as the theater stage: "Concealing his [Pierre] labored respiration, he wiped his hands long and carefully with a red handkerchief, while the spider as the youngest member of the circus family, performed a simple trick above his web" (*IB* 97—98). With strong implications of putting on a show, Pierre and the spider seem to be both in the circus, one playing at the front and the other in the background. The theatricality is further extended when "the door softly swung open, there entered—in jack boots, with a whip, powdered and spotlit with blinding violet light—the circus director [the prison director actually]" (*IB* 98). When the performance is over, "he [the prison director] ···gave a little start and in obvious distress, left the box. And thus the performance ended" (*IB* 99). The unreal atmosphere painted on Pierre and prison director along with the spider who is ridiculed by the narrator as the "official friend of the jailed" (*IB* 72) can be seen in many other places of the book. Pierre's "chalk-white face", the "painted swine" (*IB* 48) —the prisoner director, his "wax-glossy forehead", his wig "glossy as new", wearing a pink waxy flower with a speckled mouth in his button-hole" (*IB* 48), along with the family-in-law's bringing the furniture to the interview with Cincinnatus are all tinged with a strong sense of artificiality. The most theatrical thing is in the preparation of the written record of the beheading by the lawyer, the director and the executioner. We can read things such as "the programme" of the execution, "Thriller Square," as the execution place, "Adults···admitted," "Circus subscription stubs···be honored," "the performer of the execution···in red pantaloons" (*IB* 151).

Further than that, these sham characters all share this or that similarities in their appearances, their behaviors, their dresses and their character traits. Sometimes, it is even hard for the readers to distinguish one from the other since the name of one person is also used for another person in the same contextual scene and it is not a rare occurrence for two persons sharing one name or two persons sharing one same trait in one scene. In the first chapter when the death sentence is announced, "the defense counsel and the prosecutor, both wearing makeup and looking very much alike" (*IB* 19) are thus described identical with each other against the individualities of Cincinnatus. Among the three persons that Cincinnatus has to confront in the cell are the director Rodrig Ivanovich, the jailer Rodion, and the lawyer Roman Vissarinonovich. With names both starting with letter "R", the three are in some occasions interchangeable. In Chapter Three, when the three along with Cincinnatus file out to the terrace, the narrator tells us that "the lawyer's back was soiled with chalk" (*IB* 37). But when they file back, the narrator says "the back of the director's frock coat was soiled with chalk" (*IB* 38). In this case, in the same scene, the same trait occurs to two people. This only proves that they are one and the same, all flat characters part and particle of social automatons. Approaching the end of the book when Cincinnatus is about to be executed, Pierre, director and the lawyer, "without any make-up, without padding and without wigs…they turned out to resemble each other, and their identical heads moved identically on their thin necks" (*IB* 177). Casting away all the deceptive make-up, they come from one and same cruel institution that can never tolerate Cincinnatus's difference.

In addition, when reading the part describing the daughter of director Emmie, the reader will find that the same description appears again three pages later when Marthe is described: both Marthe and Emmie are described as "mere child" and "childlike" (*IB* 36/39) and their "pink mouth slightly open" (*IB* 24/39). Marthe also shares many similarities with the spider when they are both said to have velvet like things with them. In a place the narrator even speaks directly "the velvet spider, somehow resembling Marthe" (*IB* 29). Marthe is also in a way connected with the prison staff when she "used to sing that same dashing song once," the song that Rodion was singing in his bass-baritone..." (*IB* 26) When Rodrig the director is seen " in pajamas and was all in strips" (*IB* 50), while in the first person narration, Cincinnatus says "I am here through an error—not in this prison, specifically—but in this whole terrible, striped world" (*IB* 78), we have very good reasons to believe that Nabokov means to say that these sham people are not only related with each other without distinctions but also related with the mundane world that stifles the very individualities and differences of Cincinnatus whose incoming beheading is met with excitement and smile of the people in the mundane.

Sharing more or less identical traits in a strongly painted artificial theatricality, these masked characters, all standing opposite to Cincinnatus's true individuality, embody a particular kind of vulgarity known in Russian as *poshlost*. *Poshlost* is a Russian word that Nabokov introduces into English language (preferring to call it as *poshlust*). There is a series of gradual expansion and explanation on the concept of *poshlost* since this concept is not a mere label but an aesthetic judgment and a moral indictment on the part of Nabokov. (Alexandrov, *The Garland Companion to VN* 629) In his book *Nikolai Gogol* (1944), Nabokov uses ten-page writing to refer *poshlost* to the broad range of cultural, social, and political phenomena under the category of "inferior taste" (*NG* 63). He says:

> The Russian language is able to express by means of one pitiless word the idea of a certain widespread defect for which I happen to know possess no special term···English words expressing several, although by no means all aspects of *poshlust* are for instance: "cheap, sham, common···in bad taste, ···inferior, sorry, trashy···" and others under "cheapness." ···All these however suggest merely certain false values for the detection of which no particular shrewdness is required··· But what Russians call *poshlust* is beautifully timeless and so cleverly painted all over with protective tints that its presence (in a book, in a soul, in a thousand other places) often escapes detection. (*NG* 63—64)

In his 1950 lecture on "Philistines and Philistinism," Nabokov expanded the concept to a mental essence that emanates from a "smug philistine," a "dignified vulgarian," a "bourgeois" (in a Flaubertian, not a Marxist sense—for it reflects "a state of mind, not a state of pocket") (*LRL* 309). However, the main domain of *poshlost* is art and literature where Nabokov focuses on cases "when the sham is not obvious and when the values it mimics are considered, rightly or wrongly, to belong to the very highest level of art, thought or emotion⋯*poshlost* is not only the obvious trashy but also the falsely important, the falsely beautiful, the falsely clever, the falsely attractive" (*LRL* 13).

Poshlost is best embodied in M'sieur Pierre. Under the disguise of a fellow prisoner, He, the executioner in reality, is claimed to have "a rare combination of outward sociability and inward delicacy, the art of causerie and the ability to keep silent, playfulness and seriousness" (*IB* 35). He tries to make Cincinnatus a friend of him by showing to him card tricks that do not work, pathetic jokes, and chess games where he obviously cheats. In talking with Cincinnatus, he tends to be didactic and is ready any time for pontification with his second-class, smug mediocrities he finds in his life. For example, when he lists out pleasures in life in an attempt to assimilate Cincinnatus to like what everybody else likes and be moved by the things that move everybody else, he gives only general commonsense description of the things around: "The chest expands and breaths deep on such a day, when the birdies sing, and the first modest leaves appear on the first trees. Everything rejoices, everything is jubilant" (*IB* 130). And this mediocre, dish-water description is even made worse when the director's immediate comments of it as "a masterful description of April." When describing "gastronomic pleasures," he gives a grotesque combination of the things that proves nothing but his bad taste: "See the best varieties of fruit hanging from tree branches; see the butcher and his helpers dragging a pig, squealing as if it were being slaughtered; see, on the pretty plate, a substantial chunk of white lard" (*IB* 131).

The *poshlost* in its most ridiculous form is in the introduction of Pierre as Cincinnatus's "friend." As Pierre explains it, his benevolent society would like the executioner and the condemned man to develop an "atmosphere of warm camaraderie" for "the success of our common undertaking" (*IB* 128). Unsatisfied with beheading its victim in a common way, the society is now trying to make the victim show gratitude for the intimacy shown to him by the executioner. And Pierre the executioner goes so far as to make Cincinnatus somebody as his spouse or lover. Unfortunately, his social fraud ridiculously conducted is only viewed by those in the prison and the mass outside as a show, a performance, a treat that excites and entertains. Exposing the *poshlost* to a dramatic spotlight of theatricality in book, Nabokov pushes the *poshlost* onto the forefront of the stage, ridiculing and mocking at its second-class, mediocre quality of vulgarity that muffles the true and individualist perception of the world on the part of Cincinnatus, the sole real individual that cherishes a true life and a true love, the precious and the passing.

Cincinnatus's awakening does not come at a stroke and it is accompanied with a series of deceptions. Hoping that someone might come to his rescue and that his wife might show at least some sympathy to him, he is anxiously expecting when a knock at wall is heard or when an interview with his wife is arranged. As an unavoidable process of growth to undergo for gaining enlightenment and awakening, Cincinnatus must learn to stop "inspire [ing] the meaningless with meaning, and the lifeless with life" (*IB* 130). The people he trusts all turn out to be cheaters who amuse themselves by incurring suffering and pain on him. For example, when he found that Emmie, the mischievous daughter, draws a series of illustration in the first page of the book brought in by the librarian, he began to dream of escape, especially when the persistent knocking of the wall really comes. But it turns out to be Emmie's summer vacation trick made to kill time. Marthe, Cincinnatus's wife, also the addressee of the letter that Cincinnatus wrote from the first day he was in the cell, is the ultimate person who inspires Cincinnatus to record his thoughts and his understanding of the world. Among the words written, Cincinnatus recalls his romantic meeting with Marthe who was at the age of 15 at Tamara Gardens. He believes that Marthe, although betraying him from the first year of their marriage, seeing other men and giving birth to the children whose fathers are everyone else but Cincinnatus, will feel poignant at his coming death and has a compassion for his suffering. But she cruelly betrays him by alternating the arranged interview with lovemaking with the prison director. Even Cincinnatus's mother, who possesses "that ultimate, secure, all-explaining … spark … the spark proclaimed such a tumult of truth" (*IB* 116) came to Marthe after the interview with Cincinnatus to entreat Marthe to write a contract saying that there is no relationship between her as the mother and Cincinnatus the son.

Deeply buried in the theatricality of the everyday mundane trivialities, Cincinnatus, to continue living in this world, has to resort to various strategies to invent a space where holds everything he believes to be genuine, real and blissful. His life before the imprisonment was dotted with self-conscious construction of dreams, the temporary forgetting of his physical body, and making a double to trans-cross between the mundane and the imaginary space. After being put to the cell, he starts writing a letter to Marthe to reconstruct the life of the otherworld he has been leading so as to awaken her and to make her understand him. The Tamara Garden he presented in the letter is derived from both their past romance with Marthe and Cincinnatus's creative construction of a timeless world. In comparing the mundane with the otherworld, Cincinnatus gradually comes to possess a sharper and firmer consciousness to inscribe his self in his narrative.

II   The Otherworld

Cincinnatus is firm in believing in the existence of the otherworld: "It exists, my dream world, it must exist, since, surely there must be an original of the clumsy copy. Dreamy, round, and blue, it turns slowly towards me" (*IB* 80). With the meticulously depicted mundane world as its backdrop, the dreamy, metaphysical otherworld is sure to exist in a very vague, hazy, foggy way, high above the ruled, definitively defined and unimaginative earthly life. To locate the otherworld in Cincinnatus's imagination, we find in the second last chapter—Chapter 19 something that summarizes the evolution of the otherworld. There Cincinnatus says "I think I shall yet be able to express it all— the dreams, the coalescence, the disintegration" (*IB* 175). It can serve as a

guideline for us to reverse our reading to the beginning of the book to see the e-
volution of Cincinnatus's deliverance of his otherworld; at the same time, we
the reader can resemble Cincinnatus to reconstruct the otherworld in our reading
and enjoy the reward of discovering its true version. Although he uses three
words which are not directly relevant to what the otherworld is like, he has, at
least, summarized the process of his formation of it.

When the otherworldliness first appears in the book, it takes the form of
Tamara Gardens, the public park where "Marthe, when she was a bride when
she was frightened of the frogs and cockchafers⋯There, where, whenever life
seemed unbearable, one could roam, with a meal of chewed lilac bloom in
one's mouth and firefly tears in one's eyes" (*IB* 17—18). However, this Tamara Gardens that Cincinnatus's double has wandered when Cincinnatus's own self
is confined in the cell is buried deep in the narrative of the mundane world (the
narrative leads his double to the self's own house where Marthe and his her children live). With a spark of the otherworldliness, Tamara Gardens narrated here
turns out to be only one of the clumsy copies of the original one. Before the original copy appears in the eighth chapter, different clumsy copies in various contexts occur three times along with the above mentioned one. After the original
copy is presented, Tamara Gardens appears for a last time when approaching
the end of the book—in Chapter 17 when Cincinnatus is able to create the real
copy with his own independent imaginative power achieved through series of setbacks and depressions in the mundane.

Changing with each context, the otherworld in Cincinnatus's imagination
takes different forms. The first comparatively clear depiction of Tamara Gardens
appears in Cincinnatus's dream/doze the first day in the cell:

> Where, for no reason, the willows weep into three brooks⋯and the
> brooks in three cascades, each with its own small rainbow, tumble into
> the lake, where a swan floats arm in arm with its reflection. The level
> lawns, the rhododendrons, the oak groves, the merry gardeners⋯some
> grotto, some idyllic bench, on which three jokers had left three neat little
> heaps⋯some baby deer, bounding into the avenue and before your very

eyes turning into trembling mottles of sunlight——that is what those gardens were like! (*IB* 25)

The dreamy and paradise-like Garden takes a three-dimensional depiction rather than the flat two-dimensional linear description as if it is a painting in front of us: the level lawns, the rhododendrons, the deer, bench, gardener, lake, brook, willow, grove, swan, rainbow, mottles of sunlight. The things are arranged in perspective and they form different special spheres horizontally and vertically. Things are connected with each other in a most harmonious way: the willows into the brooks above which the rainbows suspend; the brooks tumbling into a lake up above which the swan flies arm in arm with its reflection on the lake. Time in its physical and commonsense in the mundane world seem nonexistent to the creatures in the otherworld. They act according to some mysterious rhythms or orders inexplicable and inaccessible to the people and things in the mundane world. There are no obvious boundaries or fixed lines dividing things up into categories or dead lifeless sections; no human or earthly logic or reason that can be resorted to explain things and creatures in Tamara Gardens: Willows merging into the brooks, rainbows arched above the cascades, swan with its water image, deer bouncing into sunlight. The whole Tamara Gardens seems to be a round space where parts merge into parts, forming a whole dreamy, round and blue world.

Apart from the objects described in Tamara Gardens, the narrative style changes here in comparison with the other parts of the narration of the book. The normal sentence structure (subject plus verbal part) is rarely seen here, only the juxtapositions of nouns and noun phrases. Besides it, even if the verb is used, they are not at the center of the sentence, but taking the gerund form that is attached to the nouns. Only one verbal part is used in the sentence of talking about the three jokers. The use of the gerund indicates that things in here are moving in an eternal way without stop; and the movement of the objects in the otherworld is a constant state in this dreamy space. In addition, the juxtaposition of the objects pushes the things to the foreground and it is the thing-in-itself that is highlighted and their poetic immortality is thus delivered. Right after the descriptions of what Tamara Gardens are like, the love scene cherished by Cincinnatus with Marthe is recalled: "There, there is Marthe's lisping prattle, her white stockings and velvet slippers, her cool breast and her rosy kisses of wild strawberries" (*IB* 25). As this copy along with the above mentioned one is connected with Marthe, they, upon reading reversely, are seen by both the readers and Cincinnatus to be clumsy copies of the original since the one important element constructed there—love is connected with a woman who later completely disillusionized Cincinnatus.

Another impure copy of Tamara Gardens is being related with a landscape painting, hanged inside the semblance of a window—a glazed recess, a showcase. In the painting, "everything was reproduced fairly accurately as far as grouping and perspective was concerned···were it not for the drab colors, the stirless treetops and the torpid lighting" (*IB* 65). Here in the painting, Cincinnatus tries to imagine "gazing through an embrasure ··· recognized those avenues···groves, the portico at the right, the detached poplars···the unconvincing blue of the lake, the pale blob that was probably a swan" (*IB* 65). Though Cincinnatus imaginatively constructed his Tamara Gardens through the objects in the painting, he also recognizes this version: "all of this was somehow not fresh, antiquated, covered with dust, and the glass through which Cincinnatus was looking bore smudges, from some of which a child's hand could be reconstructed" (*IB* 65). The smudges of a child's hand in this context surely belong to Emmie, who draws illustrations that hint at helping Cincinnatus's escape from the cell. Finding out later that it is only Emmie's mischievous whim to entertain herself for her summer vacation, Cincinnatus finds that this version of Tamara Gardens is contaminated with the hand smudges of the child, deceivingly enchanting him to go to his otherworld.

Related with those deceptive figures such as Marthe and Emmie, Tarmara Gardens, impure as it is, inspires Cincinnatus to seek for the real, original copy. His active and positive construction, no longer handicapped by those mundane figures, takes more metaphysical form in Chapter Eight and promises more power on the part of Cincinnatus. Here Tamara Gardens is mentioned for the last time since afterwards Cincinnatus is able to construct the original copy with his own independent awakening. In Chapter Eight, Cincinnatus set himself a task, "a task of not now and not here…Not here! The horrible 'here'" (*IB* 79). Realizing that there is some possibility of an original copy of his formerly constructed otherworld upon the here and the now, Cincinnatus shows further in his letter what should be included in his otherworld:

> The misty air gradually clears, and it is suffused with such radiant, tremulous kindness…*There, tam, la-bas*, the gaze of men glows with in-imitable understanding; *there* the freaks that are tortured here walk unmo-lested; *there* time takes shape according to one's pleasure … *There, there* are the originals of those gardens where we used to roam and hide in this world; *there* everything strikes one by its bewitching evidence, by the sim-plicity of perfect good; *there* everything pleases one's soul…filled with the kind of fun that children know; *there* shines the mirror that now and then sends a chance reflection here. (*IB* 80)

Thus, Cincinnatus's otherworld is a moral place of goodness, perfection, timelessness enjoyed by people who are equal and who can understand the lan-guage and the secret of the otherworld that people of this side of the world have no such sensibility and imagination to perceive. In this description, the meta-physical is related with the aesthetics and the ethics. The moral goodness evokes the aesthetic bliss and pleasure. In turn, the timeless space eternalizes and im-mortalizes beauty and human love. But it is not an empty utopia-like otherworld deprived of the mundane. It reflects the life in this world.

To trace Cincinnatus's awakening process of self as related with his con-struction of the otherworld, we can seek for guidance from the letter Cincinnatus writes: "I think I shall yet be able to express it all—the dreams, the coales-cence, the disintegration" (*IB* 175). These three words enable the readers to follow in a reverse order how he constructs his otherworld through dreams, coa-lescence and the disintegration. Before being put into the cell, Cincinnatus, "ever since early childhood [,] has had dreams" (*IB* 78). The dreams "enno-bled and spiritualized" (*IB* 78) the world. He can, in his sleep or in a hot bath, where he can temporarily forget the physical confinement of the body, enjoy in his self-created otherworld versions the bliss of the otherworld. Some other times, he can close his eyes and let his double transcend his own self and go to that imaginative sphere of otherworld when the mundane life proves intolerable. He writes that he has

> long since grown accustomed to the thought that what we call dreams is semi-reality, the promise of reality, a foreglimpse and a whiff of it···that is they contain, in a vague, diluted state, more genuine reality than our vaunted waking life which···is semi-sleep, an evil drowsiness. (*IB* 78)

When he is in the cell and puts himself in a writing state, he is self-consciously recording and recreating his understandings of both the mundane and the otherworld. With different versions of Tamara Gardens in different contexts and his hesitations and unsureness of what a real otherworld is like, Cincinnatus distills and crystallizes them along his process of awakening through his detached watching of the people around him, meditating and writing. By Chapter 17, Cincinnatus is seen "exploring the surroundings with a diligent eye, he easily removed the murky film of night from the familiar lawns and···erased from them the superfluous lunar dusting, so as to make them exactly as they were in his memory" (*IB* 160). Writing enables him to strive to put the ideas into words so that thought and expression can be united as one. By accumulating the different versions of his Tamara Gardens and covering one version onto the other, the confinement of the prison of time is thus broken and the process of writing immortalizes the original copy of his otherworld. This is what he does with the coalescence.

The disintegration comes after the original copy of otherworld is constructed. He writes his realization in his letter at the end of the book:

> Everything has duped me—all of this theatrical, pathetic stuff···and I should not have sought salvation within its confines···I have discovered the little crack in life; here it broke off, where it had once been soldered to

something else, something genuinely alive, important and vast … Within this irreparable little crack decay has set in. (*IB* 175)

The crack in life is the place through which the otherworld truth can be glimpsed at and the wind from the otherworld can blow into this world. Looking at this world through the other side of life and death, Cincinnatus realizes that the disintegration of this confinement of this world is a must for him to enjoy full freedom of wondering at the original otherworld he constructed since the break of this world is soldered to something else, something genuinely alive, important and vast. The first chapter sees that Cincinnatus writes the words that "after all I had premonitions, has premonitions of this finale" (*IB* 12). In the last chapter, the narrator says that his awakening "was presaged by barely noticeable phenomena, by the peculiar effects on everyday implements, by a certain general instability, by a certain flaw in all visible matter" (*IB* 183). After a series of dreams and coalescences, the narrator says: "Plaster began to fall from a ceiling. A crack described a tortuous course across the wall. The cell, no longer needed, was quite obviously disintegrating" (*IB* 180). These summarizing words of the narrator make meaningful and important Cincinnatus's maturity of the self as related to the spiritual construction of the otherworld. Pinned in-between the two worlds and after the testing of the self, he is now fully prepared for the otherworld, with the mundane that now needs to be discarded.

The enlightenment of Cincinnatus is encouraged by the appearance of a moth. The fabulous moth is brought in by Rodion to feed the spider in the cell but it eludes the jailer. This episode serves as a powerful message of encouragement for Cincinnatus and it is inspirational in several ways. First, the moth, struggling against Rodion's attempt to make it a meek victim of the spider, represents Cincinnatus's independence achieved at the end of the book. Second, the way that the moth disappeared "as if the very air had swallowed it" (*IB* 174) hints at a link at Cincinnatus and the moth. Third, far from being an obedient and crudely made toy spider, this moth is ardently alive and is beautifully formed with forever-open eyes on the visionary wings and its enchanting appearance (Connolly, *Nabokov's Invitation to a Beheading* 16). Fourth, the vital vibration of the moth's wings is a strong echo of Cincinnatus's: "that primordial palpitation of mine" and "how I wriggled out, slippery, naked," (*IB* 77) just like a moth from the cocoon. When Cincinnatus is longing for the otherworld, he always feels that his heart is like a feather, a sign connected with "the brown fuzz [that] had struck to the edge of the table where the moth had quivered only a short time ago" (*IB* 176). The coming of the moth appears at the crucial moment in the development of Cincinnatus's awakening and his ultimate stage of independence. As what Connolly has said about the significance of the moth, the appearance of the moth may in some mysterious way facilitate Cincinnatus's understanding of the correct path he must follow. (17) In Nabokov's early story "Christmas," (1924) he uses the moth to indicate a sign that not all is lost with death and that the spirit remains inviolable and immortal. In that little story, the protagonist Sleptsov is full of grief of the death of his son and is contemplating suicide. But when he is sorting out the things left by his son, he is startled by some snapping sound. It belongs to a huge moth that has evolved itself from a cocoon kept by his son before his death, a cocoon that the father has believed containing only a dead chrysalid. The appearance is a sure sign in Nabokov's art of the existence of spirit and immortality of the otherworld.

III   The Interconnection Between the Mundane and the Otherworld

Nabokov's otherworld sensibility is not an empty concept that contains dry metaphysical elements. Nor is it an unreal utopia that excludes the mundane and the real world. Rather, the two are being closely related with each other with one being higher than the other. And at the same time, the mundane is again the springboard for the characters in the novels to transport themselves to another perspective to see more clearly the mundane from the other side of this world. Dominated by trivialities, commonsense knowledge, utilitarian world view, the mundane world with its stark reality sets a contrast against character's consciousness and self-awareness of the existence of another space where happiness, love and immortality reign. With one down-to-earth and the other enchanting and imaginative, the two worlds complement each other by providing differ-ent spaces for the characters to cross-over the boundaries for a truer perception of their living conditions. The entanglement between the two worlds are seen re-flecting each other and connected with each other through various devices such as the repeated occurrence of a same sign, the creation of a double (the free crossing-over of the character back and forth between the two spaces), the two narratives (Cincinnatus's narration in the letter and narrator's presentation of the story) inter-echoing with each other. Nabokov knows only too well that only the substantiality of the one world can make the other stand out in its poetic, insub-stantial and enchanting way. And his love of the details, his exactness in the de-piction of the trivialities and his profound concern with a better world combined to enable him to wriggle out the truth of life from the very mundane details of the mass culture. Designing the text in the interconnections between the two worlds, Nabokov tests either one of the two with the other as a foil so as to exert control upon his meticulously created artistic space that incorporates the two.

　　The mundane world and the otherworld are two consciously constructed spaces by Nabokov. As an artist, he re-appropriates the spaces of the mundane and the otherworld as representational spaces that speak and that are alive. Representational space in the artistic works does not actually change the con-struction of a city, a house, or a dwelling, but rather it results in symbolic and artistic productions. In realistic writing, the places as the house and the bed-room are delivered as a place where nothing moves except for discourses itself, which, like a camera panning over a scene, moves over the whole panorama (qtd. in Thacker 32). Unlike the places in realistic writing, the spaces depicted by the modern writers like Nabokov contain some elements belonging to other spaces or enclose other spaces in it through movement. Thus, the concept of space is different from that of the place. Space indicates a sense of movement, of history, of becoming, while place is often thought to imply a static sense of location, of being, or of dwelling. (Thacker 13) Thus, the street, the hou-ses, the gardens and places with geometrical dimension are transformed into spaces by the people walking there, living there, and producing spaces with their life practices. People as acting and moving subject connected different spaces. Of course, there is no clear-cut distinction between space and place and they combine to form sites where events and activities are performed. But the flux of the spaces in modern writing is foregrounded. In this way, the spaces are transformed into heterotopias whose major feature is the combination of the material and the metaphorical and the important point is that "heterotopia involves a sense of movement between the real and the unreal; it is thus a site defined by a process, the stress being upon the fact that it contests another site" (Thacker 25). Seen from this perspective, the two spaces of the mundane and the otherworld, though processing different characters, are two influxes rather than fixed sites and at the same time, they embed within each other, ready to transform itself to the other.

The sign of the mirror, making its appearance many times both in the mundane and the otherworld, connects the two spaces as a material item as well as a metaphorical one. The first appearance of the mirror is the hand-mirrors of the women of fashion who are sitting as audience in the law court where Cincinnatus's death sentence is announced. The women and Cincinnatus may well shift their roles in this context since they can both be seen as the viewer and the viewed. When Cincinnatus looks at the women with mirrors in their hands, he is the viewer who is being viewed. The mirror held by women of fashion may be a sign indicating that they, the mundane is confined in their own world, only being able to see the reflection of themselves while Cincinnatus, seeing the hand-mirror from the other side, anticipates Cincinnatus's power of possessing another perspective, perceiving the *poshlost* in the mundane from somewhere else, some other space. With this hand-mirror, the two worlds are seen at the same time from both sides of the mirror. Another appearance of mirror is in Cincinnatus's interview with his family-in-law who had brought with them the wardrobe with a mirror in it. In this interview, except for Marthe holding a hand-mirror, the mirrored wardrobe "bringing with its own private reflection (namely, a corner of the connubial bedroom with a strip of sunlight across the floor, a dropped glove, and an open door in the distance)" (*IB* 85) is brought along by the family. The wardrobe mirror's private reflection contains the reflections of the bedroom where Marthe keeps betraying Cincinnatus by sleeping with other men. The reflection of a corner of bedroom and an open door in the distance brings the space of bedroom into the cell, merging the boundaries of these two spaces. Thus denies the fixities of the two spaces in the mundane. But an imaginary space is also involved here since the reflections are what have been imagined by Cincinnatus who, in his mind's eye, seems to see a glimpse of life going on there in the bedroom. Mirror, when it reflects the things in Marthe's bedroom, it contains an unreal image of the real things in the bedroom.

Thus, in Foucault's sense of mirror, the reflections of the real things on the mirror are located nowhere, but in a virtual space. Thus, the gaze of the viewer, say this time the narrator/character, must pass through the reality of the actual glass of the mirror, and also through the unreality of the virtual image in the mirror. The real space of the mirror thus functions in a counter-real fashion (Thacker 25). Through the gaze of the narrator/character, the mirror in the wardrobe brings the unreal image of the real things in the bedroom, thus achieving the movement from the real space to the unreal space. At the same time, the reflection of the image itself transcends time and space, bringing in the reflection of the things belonging to another time and space by the narrator/character's imaginative thinking, thus also merging the boundary between the real and the imaginary. Another important appearance of mirror transcending the mundane and the otherworld is seen in Cincinnatus's realization that Tamara Gardens is only some clumsy copy of the original one. He writes in his letter "*there* shines the mirror that now and then sends a chance reflection here…" (*IB* 80) As its appearance in the space of the mundane, the mirror in the original copy of *there*, the other space (the otherworld), reflecting the real image *here* (this world of the mundane), is merging the boundaries of the real (the mundane) and the unreal (the otherworld) when it, as a real mirror, functions itself in a counter-real fashion. Looked from this sense, Tamara Gardens is also a heterotopia, containing the real as a public garden as well as the unreal and timeless that are imagined by Cincinnatus.

The creation of a double of Cincinnatus distinguishes the boundaries of the mundane and the otherworld by trans-crossing the two, but it also shows forth the indispensability of the mundane towards the otherworld. While transporting between the two worlds, the double, no matter what space he is in, self-consciously reflects and examines the other space. This otherness in the self of Cincinnatus helps him to gain a third eye to see clearly what happens around him and in his dreams, an eye that is like the eyes on the wings of the moth, open eternally. In the letter, he writes: "I have been my own accomplice, who knows too much, and therefore is dangerous···" (*IB* 76—77) This accomplice is "the gangrel, that accompanies each of us—you, and me, and him over there—doing what we would like to do at that very moment, but cannot···" (*IB* 22) This double is "the mainspring of my "I" (*IB* 77) in Cincinnatus words and can have "a free journey from fact to fantasy and return. " (*IB* 77) The free transportation between fact and fantasy, the mundane and the otherworld transforms both of the two sites into spaces, heteratopias whose important function is the establishment of the relationship of one heterotopia with another space. Rather than two fixed stabilities, static and unchanging, the mundane and the otherworld become alive and uncertain in their own rights with the frequent movement of Cincinnatus's self and his double.

On the other hand, the double reconstructs from the very mundane place an otherworldly space through its own creative imagination. Imprisoned in a fortress which "towered hugely on the crest of a huge cliff, of which it seemed to be a monstrous outgrowth," (*IB* 37) Cincinnatus is for a while brought out to the terrace outside the fortress. Here the narrator gives a description of the surroundings of the fortress as if there is a camera, panning from a high location, thus presenting a panoramic view of the landscape:

Farther away the sun-flooded town described an ample hemicycle: some of the varicolored houses proceeded in even rows, accompanied by round trees, while others, awry, crept down slopes, stepping on their own shadows; one could distinguish the traffic moving on First Boulevard ···and still further, towards the hazy folds of the hills that formed the horizon, there was the dark stipple of oak groves···while other bright ovals of water gathered, glowing···over to the west. (*IB* 37)

This discourse lists the things in the landscape around the fortress in a static way, presenting a map of the surroundings in the mundane world. This kind of description for Michel de Certeau is applied not to a space but to a place, implying an indication of stability because for de Certeau, the description of the space is achieved through a set of actions. (Thacker 31) And a paragraph later, Cincinnatus "made a complete tour of the terrace" and "his eyes were making highly illegal excursions" (*IB* 38). After completing his trip, he returned to its south parapet: "Now he thought he distinguished that very bush in flower, that bird, that path disappearing under a canopy of ivy—" (*IB* 38). The map-like description is transformed by Cincinnatus through his tour into an imaginary space where he can distinguish from the very mundane world the bush, that bird, that path he cherished in his dreamy otherworld.

The narration of the narrator and the narration of Cincinnatus as presented in his letter are interlacing with each other. These two versions of narrations that constitute the whole book echo in some ways. The narrator's narration combines both the external events of the novel and Cincinnatus's inner conflictions with the outside world. The external events involving those people and things around Cincinnatus are narrated in a matter of fact way with a strong sense of theatricality. For those passages that involve Cincinnatus's inner thoughts, the narrator seems to share the sensibilities of Cincinnatus in the mundane world and render them in a free indirect discourse, merging the lines between the narrator and Cincinnatus the character. With already these two layers enveloping the innermost thoughts that are uttered by the letter, the letter is delivered in the first person narration, sometimes addressing to Cincinnatus himself, most of the time to Marthe, an addressee that Cincinnatus never managed to send the letter and never succeeded to make his meaning understood. Embedded in the core of the whole narration, the letter conjoins both the mundane and the otherworld, creating, constructing and synthesizing his innermost thoughts in verbal form. But there is one point that can not be neglected. In the narrator's narration, we can also find Cincinnatus's inner thoughts that have spoken aloud or in some other times, we see Cincinnatus is speaking to himself. In addition, sometimes, Cincinnatus's words in the letter are directly and immediately commented by the narrator. In this way, one narrative is extended to another very naturally and the narrations conducted by the two are combined to constitute a synthesis of narrations of both the mundane and the otherworld.

IV   Cincinnatus the Writer VS. Nabokov the Speaking Self

In the above three sections, we see the evolutionary process of Cincinnatus as a character in the narration and a character who himself attempts to write a letter in his 19-day-stay in the cell to his beloved woman to express his fears, longings and enlightenments. The quotations from Cincinnatus's letter in the above three sections are used to interpret his maturing process as a character who eventually finds the right direction for him to follow. But in this section, Cincinnatus as a conscious writer who strives to find the right words for his thoughts is discussed in relation with Nabokov the writer.

But before we come to Cincinnatus's writing practice—the letter, we need to direct our attentions first to some important details that can be combined to form some unexpected relationships and meanings. When we read carefully the text, we find from the narrator that from the very beginning Cincinnatus is expecting his awakening. The series of awakening appear in various degrees and stages and are accompanied by various voices. The voices, sometimes as doomed din of voices, sometimes as the deceptive knocking of the wall, all at first fail to be correctly recognized by Cincinnatus. Only when Cincinnatus is on the verge of being beheaded on the execution block while the outside world goes disintegrated does he recognize the real voices of the beings akin to him. According to the narrator in the last chapter, Cincinnatus understands that this very awakening he is all the way expecting "was presaged by barely noticeable phenomena, by the peculiar effects on everyday implements, by a certain general instability, by a certain flaw in all visible matter" (*IB* 183). Only one chapter earlier, Cincinnatus as a writer writes the last word of the letter "death" and then crosses out this word, thinking of some words with greater precision: " 'execution', perhaps, 'pain' or 'parting' ——something like that" (*IB* 176).

While meditating for the right word, immediately following this, Cincinnatus notices the brown fuzz that is left by the moth. He went to stroke the moth. The moth is not awakened. Then Cincinnatus's letter ends here abruptly with the coming of the executioner for his final moment. The writing of Cincinnatus disappears, dissolving into the very air as the moth disappears from the jailer's hands. But when the jailer cannot find where the moth has gone, Cincinnatus knows—he knows from where the mighty vibration of the wings of the moth is produced, which differs from that of the clock (the voices of the mundane). Following the voices that might be produced by the vibration of the now awakened moth (which is not awaken by Cincinnatus's stroke after Cincinnatus's writing of the word "death"), Cincinnatus, like the moth's shedding off the brown fuzz, shed off the mundane burdens along with the word "death", walking to the directions of the right voices.

From the above presentation of some important details, we can figure out the relationships among the voices as related to the narrator's narration, Cincinnatus's own letter-writing and the moth (represented as the otherworld concern). The narrator in the novel is a third-person narrator who is different from the mundane people and shares Cincinnatus's sensibility of the existence of the otherworld. The narrator is even insightful to know that Cincinnatus has an otherness, a double which combines with the self of Cincinnatus to form a complete self. In narrator's eyes, the shifting between the self and his double causes the great difference of Cincinnatus from the other ordinary people and the spiritual part of Cincinnatus that is gaining over the fleshy part is part of Cincinnatus's maturation. With such an insightful standing point, the narrator commands many narrative devices: pure narration with impartial attitude, free indirect discourse (FID) that shares the characters' consciousness and sensibility while merging the boundary between the narrator's words and the character's words, free direct discourse (FDD) that conveys Cincinnatus's inner thoughts spoken aloud. When we reread the book with Cincinnatus's letter as a starting point, that is, to read only his letter in a successive way while skipping the pure narrations and dialogues, we find that among the letter's surrounding narrative text, the most subjective narration or the narration closest to Cincinnatus's direct discourse is direct discourse, that is, Cincinnatus's direct thoughts in quotation marks. Then the less direct discourse found surrounding Cincinnatus's letter is FID, the narration conducted by the narrator but whose narration can go into the consciousness of Cincinnatus to perceive the thoughts there. The only difference from the above mentioned one is that there is no quotation mark, thus merging the boundary between the narrator and the character since the words said have a strong sense of character's understanding of the world. And the most objective discourse surrounding the letter is the pure narration of the narrator narrating in a matter-of-fact way.

Buried deep in various narrative discourses ranking from the most subjective to the most objective, Cincinnatus's verbal narration constitutes the innermost core of the whole narration from the beginning to the end of the book. From narrative perspective, his letter is a message of the utmost importance that the author intends to transfer. First, the narrator who could have well delivered the thoughts and ideas in Cincinnatus's mind gives the right of direct utterance to the character and lets the character speak out his ideas. The freedom that has been assigned to the character enables Cincinnatus to hear his own voice in a clearer way so that he may one day come to his final enlightenment. Second, Cincinnatus's letter is not presented in a place once and for all. Rather it is relayed with the other narrative discourses such as dialogues, pure narration, FID, FDD. Besides, the whole letter is fragmented and scattered in different stages. This proves that the letter is of high importance to the maturation of Cincinnatus's consciousness and it facilities his different stages of evolution of thoughts and understanding of this world and the otherworld. Third, Cincinnatus in the letter stresses the difficulties of delivering what the otherworld is like and stammers and repeats a lot solely for the purpose of putting the secret of the otherworld in his mind into words. And this very effort is strongly echoed by the narrator's pure narration, FID and FDD, which offer the development of Cincinnatus's observance of the outside world. Cincinnatus's very effort of showing forth his subjective struggling for the right words to express his difficult ideas also complements the narrator's comparatively objective narration. Casting off the narratives layer by layer, we find the hardest truth is contained in the letter in which Cincinnatus strives with great efforts to transfer and deliver what he, only he, knows about the truth of this world and the secret concerning somewhere else—the otherworld. In writing the letter, Cincinnatus confronts some difficulties: 1) Is there time enough for him to finish what he wants to say? 2) How does one put thoughts to words in an exact way? That is, in Cincinnatus's case, how can one use the language of this world to express the idea of the otherworld? Or how does one speak to people who do not understand the language used in the letter? 3) Is there an audience who read and understand the letter if it can not be sent to Marthe the addressee? 4) What is the efficient way to write so as to best express one's thoughts: the poet's way or other literary devices?

Time is one important element that confines Cincinnatus from the freedom he yearns for. Along with other signs such as cell, bars in the window, the shadow of Cincinnatus's ribs reflected on the wall and walls themselves, time imprisons men and there is no escapement. Being fully conscious of the time imprisonment, Cincinnatus knows that he is like all the other mortals, not knowing his mortal hour and thus is yet to remove the last film of fear. But before casting off his final film of fear, he in his letter shatters the time imprisonment by transferring an idea that in the otherworld "*there* time takes shape according to one's pleasure, like a figured rug whose folds can be gathered in such a way that two designs will meet—and the rug is once again smoothed out, and you live on, or else superimpose the next image on the last, endlessly, endlessly⋯" (*IB* 80) Rather than being a slave of the prison of time, one can invent his own time according to his own pleasure. By covering one image upon another on and on in an endless way, one breaks the linear procession of time and immortalizes the images cherished through synchronization—freely combining the past, the present and the future into one particular moment. And that moment transcends the clock-time of the mundane world and creates around itself a vacuum of intensive joy and bliss that is repeatedly echoed and expressed in Nabokov's own art. Embedded amid the rings of the prison clock, Cincinnatus's letter is either preceded or followed by the narration of the vibrations and ringing of time from the clock on the cell wall warning of the mundane. This conscious arrangement draws attention to and a demarcation line between the two worlds: the world as a prison confined by time and an artistic world created by Cincinnatus's art of writing in his letter. His letter thus offers a promise of immortality that can be achieved through his verbal art.

Cincinnatus's longing for the right words for his thoughts is seen very keenly in his eagerly written letter. Confined by the cliché expressions for trite ideas, he attempts in his letter a unique combination of the common words for expressing new meanings. Through uncommon combination of the commonplace words, they can come alive and "share their neighbor's sheen, heat, shadow, while reflecting itself in its neighbor and renewing the neighboring words in the process, so that the whole line is live iridescence" (*IB* 79). While attempting to explain his ideas of the dreamy, round and blue world, Cincinnatus uses negation, that is, proposing a way of expression and then immediately deny it and then try another way and negate it again. The repeated negation makes minus plus minus become a plus. All these explanations seem to combine to express his meanings. However, like what Cincinnatus says in the letter: "Brought up into the air, the word bursts, as burst those spherical fishes that breathe and blaze only in the compressed murk of the depths when brought up in the net" (*IB* 80). That compressed murk of the depths is the place that holds the soul. It is sure to be distorted and impossible to be expressed by the fleshy words, words that have all been contaminated by the mediocre thoughts and ideas in the mundane. Thus, by negating and repeating, Cincinnatus increases the strength of his description while hinting at the fact that his otherworld is all that are said but more than those all.

Like all the writers, Cincinnatus is also concerned about having a reader for his message. At first, the letter is meant to write for Marthe. But it dawns upon Cincinnatus that Marthe, like all the other people in this world, can not be hoped to understand his words: "as there is in the world not a single human who can speak; or, even more simply, not a single human; I must think only of myself, of that force which urges me to express myself" (*IB* 81). Echoing Nabokov's concern with a sui generis art for creative readers, Cincinnatus resorts to all the images, metaphors, repeatedly but at the same time cosmically draws connections of the things from all different perspectives. To understand them all is very demanding. Only the really creative readers can figure out the true meaning while not being trapped by the superficial meanings. To be a real creative reader to understand Cincinnatus's letter, one has to have imagination, an imagination that can creatively associate all the scattering details and synthesize them in such a way that they combine to reveal hidden meanings. To perceive the true meaning, one needs to look for the cracks, or the hiatus among the words for that glimmer. As a creative writer, though claiming having no training for putting ideas into words, Cincinnatus is that kind of good artist that Nabokov affirms, the artist whose creative thrill comes from "a sudden live image constructed in a flash out of dissimilar units which are apprehended all at once in a stellar explosion of the mind" (*LL* 379).

As Nabokov's most favorite novel in Russian, *Invitation to a Beheading* was composed in the mid-1930. In several of his works done in this period, he shows "his dismay over the Soviet regime in his former homeland and his apprehension about the rising tide of prejudice and repression in his current place of residence, Germany" (Connolly, *Nabokov's Invitation to a Beheading* 33). In these novels and short stories, Nabokov expressed his denunciation against the attempt of the collective to make an individual join in its activities that hide some malign purposes. In this agony toward the tyranny, there is the strong concern toward his father's death—killed while trying to stop a political assassination in 1922. The specter of his father's death and the hope that his father's spirit would remain a vital presence in his life informs much of Nabokov's writing. Nabokov's strong desire of "peeling off a drab and unhappy past and replacing it with a brilliant invention" (ibid. 30) is repeatedly affirmed in many of his works. Though we are not sure if the execution of Cincinnatus is performed, we know that for him death can never kill his otherworld quest and death is only one necessary step for him to shrug off the confines of this world and enter his otherworld for eternal bliss and joy.

For Nabokov, death is only the first stage of series of one's soul and his hope that death will not mean the cession of being itself is determinedly presented in various ways in his works. *The Gift*, one of Nabokov's best Russian novels, composed at the same time with *Invitation to a Beheading*, has a protagonist, Fyodor who has a vision of his missing father's return at a pivotal moment in the book. (ibid. 31) In a short story written around mid-1930, the title story "Lik" (1939) again echoes Cincinnatus as also a solitary, unappreciated individual who is disgusted at the mundane and is ready to leave this entire world behind to enter a beautiful and better otherworld. As a lonely Russian émigré working as an actor in France, Lik feels that he is pushed to live on the outskirts of life and thus is always on the verge of passing into the world of dramas he is performing and finds that there is "a world of ineffable tenderness—a bluish, delicate world where fabulous adventures of the senses occur, and unheard-of metamorphoses of the mind" (*Stories* 465). To linger long in that tenderness, Lik imagines death on the stage and for him, just as Cincinnatus is at the last moment of life: "He would not notice his death, crossing over instead into the actual world of a chance play, now blooming anew because of his arrival, while his smiling corpse lay on the board, the toe of one foot protruding from beneath the folds of the lowered curtain" (*Stories* 465).

In *Invitation to a Beheading*, as the narrator and the character who have combined to inscribe a sensibility of the existence of the otherworld and its transcendence of this side of the boundary of life and death, Nabokov believes in will to happiness in the otherworld realm. Artistic precision and creative imagination can transport one from the pains and pleasures in the past to an immortal happiness. This self-conscious recollection of one's past prepares Nabokov for an already-known realm of artistic immortality where the dead returns recurrently, in various forms, inspiring the writer to inscribe his own identity via literary illusions and deceptions. The meanings that the writer wants truly to express lie beneath those entangled details narrated by different figures, with different voices. Like Cincinnatus who discards his dress layer after layer until the hard core is left so as to express his exclusive thoughts, we the readers, after processing layer after layer of narrations conducted by different voices, finds the real voice of the writer—the hard core buried deep beneath the text. As an artistic synthesis of the past and the present of Nabokov's life in homeland and exile, *Invitation to a Beheading* dramatizes a self that is imprisoned and isolated in a fortress, whose active reconstruction of his cherished otherworld disintegrates the cell along with the mundane world and hence is rewarded with eternal bliss and happiness. A self as Nabokov, who has lost a beloved father and a beloved motherland due to political reasons, creatively reconstructs an artistic otherworld through transcending his fictional world of mundane details (details not without a glimmering of his own past life) to deliver his important message to his creatively imaginative readers. For Nabokov, one can regain the loss in an affirmative invention of another realm and reassert one's happiness by reappropriating the pains of the past.

Chapter Two   The Speaking "I" Inscribed Between Literary "Real" and Imagination in *The Real Life of Sebastian Knight*

The Real Life of Sebastian Knight, Nabokov's first English novel, was completed in 1939 and published in 1941. By now, Nabokov is a writer of a famous book—*Invitation to a Beheading* and has finished his most ambitious long Russian novel—*The Gift*. V. , the narrator of the book, is attempting to write a biography of his recently dead half-brother—Sebastian Knight; a famous novel writer. To write that biography, V. is trying hard to collect all kinds of materials about the life of Sebastian available from all possible clues: Sebastian's friends, mistresses, his secretary and books and letters written by Sebastian and other people. In this quest for Sebastian's real life, V. is more and more convinced that he shares some instincts with Sebastian and is capable of understanding and retrieving some past life episodes of Sebastian through some clues that may mean nothing to other people. In constructing Sebastian's life, V. recalls his own life which intersects with those episodes of Sebastian's while delivering his experience of procuring the materials from Sebastian's friends, mistresses and undergraduate classmates. V. also comments on Sebastian's books and quotes in some places to help him imagine or visualize some glimpses of Sebastian's real life. When the novel is near its end, V. says that Sebastian wrote a letter to him and wanted him to come for some important things to say to him. Before he decided to meet Sebastian, V. received a wire from the doctor saying that Sebastian is dying and wants to see him. But after a nightmarish traveling by train and taxi, V. still cannot manage to see him before Sebastian dies.

However, V. has his own enlightenment and is evoked by the writing of the very book. He feels that Sebastian is him and he is Sebastian. Thus, the "real" narrator gives us a "real" account of his half-brother's life, including his artistic books and his real-life lovers and at the end tells us that he is Sebastian Knight and Sebastian Knight is him. As it is narrated by a character "V." who manages to write a biography of his half-brother Sebastian Knight, many critics review the book as a self-conscious meta-fiction, a fiction about writing fictions. They focus on the stylistics and regard this merging of the two characters as a post-modern subversion of the "reality" of the realistic novels—laying bare the techniques of the realistic literary tradition, thus foregrounding its fictionality. When the book is seen merely as laying bare the writing devices and as Nabokov's another experiment of fascinating verbal styles, it is pitifully reduced to a play of literary skills to dizzy the readers while neglecting the important messages that Nabokov transfers through the characters in his book.

It is possible that V. is too involved in the biography he is undertaking to tell himself away from his character. He seems to be guided by the ghostly spirit of Sebastian and finally comes to follow some secret or uncommon truth that has been promised by Sebastian but failed to be delivered. It is also possible that V., playing the role of an artist, invented his half-brother relationship with Sebastian and all the other characters, books and letters so as to go with his cleverly wrought story. These extrapolations are all due to the uncertainties of the reliabilities of the characters who present their view points through subjective knowledge which are derived from second-hand or even third-hand sources. The narrator "V." who is supposed to be most objective of these characters/narrators is unsure of the knowledge he obtained from various sources. Even for those parts of his first-hand experiences with Sebastian, he complained that he was either too young to tell or too reserved for both of them to have better understandings of each other. If the narrator is so unreliable, let alone the validity of those characters, books, criticisms, comments, and letters embedded in his story.

Being put in such a hard-to-define situation, the readers, besides being amazed at the magical fusions of different genres and ingenious parodies of literary conventions on the part of the author—Nabokov, cannot resist the temptation to ask further questions concerning thematic meanings lying underneath. If the author is simply being concerned with laying bare the devices of composing fictions, is there any need for him to weave such a series of evasive fictional worlds, one embedded in another, further complicated by those story-tellers who evoke other story-tellers evoking still others? Therefore, if it is a mere show of verbal and stylistic devices, questions and doubts come: 1) Why are there evocative messages on the *other* side of life, messages that are supposed to be only perceived by a dying man but now understood in a way by V. ? 2) With all those constructions and reconstructions from various sources by V. , why still does Sebastian's life forever recede from us and all efforts prove to be hopelessly futile and discouraging for the version of his real life? 3) Is it only a coincidence that Sebastian and his mother die of the same disease and share the capricious and uncertain characteristics in terms of their life style and love affairs? How does one see the fatidic numbers that join father, mother and Sebastian together in fateful events in the three's lives? 4) How does one explain the scatterings of Nabokov's personal life details and his personal artistic positions concerning life, death, literary criticism and literary conventions? Are these merely reappropriations of the past or is Nabokov, wearing masks, airing his own understanding of art and artifice in the novel?

To tackle these doubts, we need to start from Nabokov's ideas of reality and otherworld sensibility. For Nabokov, reality can never exist without the quotation mark because there is no stark reality, only the reality perceived by subjective minds. Reality can not be obtained in any absolute sense. Rather, reality can only be approached nearer and nearer but can never be grasped fully. Therefore, in literary fictions, Nabokov puts his characters and events in a meticulously created "real" world, the details and trivialities derived from the real world but have been filtered through a subjective consciousness, thus smeared with a tinge of imaginative shimmering. In this way, Nabokov's "real" setting or "real" things in his novel is different from the reality and verisimilitude of the traditional novel. The world that he created for his characters to move and act is a precise world of art delineated through all five senses. The narrations of the scenes seem to be made by a person who is ready to respond to all wind and light from the outside world and open all his tentacles to absorb things around. This synaesthesia adds sensual glamour and dreamy sensibility to his scrupulously and minutely painted "real" world. Its subjectively selected details also add a sphere of strong self-consciousness into his efforts to make things strange, defamiliarizing the commonsense knowledge and conveying a new perspective to stimulate the readers to see better with increased alertness and cognitive engagement.

The creative power of the masterful author as Nabokov is not limited to this. The "real" details that should be fondled by the readers should not be perceived horizontally, but vertically. For Nabokov the great artist is also a great deceiver. If details are discussed linearly, they only form a story. But when they are seen vertically like a painting through rereading, the re-readers can be rewarded with the discoveries of patterns otherwise unseen by the careless readers who stop at the surface. The coincidences and meanings of the details can be fully enjoyed as an artistic work with an artificiality that is like the mimicry of creatures in nature, their painstaking deceptions well beyond their practical protective purposes, simply for the delight of the eye and aesthetic bliss. By transcending the superficial details, one can see the hidden meanings from the nexus carefully weaved into the artistic work. This hidden meaning is always maneuvered carefully by the author's intrusion and his creative weaving of his own concerns in the past along with his imagination (as in Nabokov's sense) into his texts so that the readers can discover a pattern thematically lying underneath. The hidden meaning, at its highest level, is that the dead is resurrected and they, through the secret knowledge, guide the living to the higher consciousness, the patterns of transcendence and otherworldly understandings of this world. The writing hand of author/character is moved by a symbiotic consciousness both in and out of this world. (Bethea 702) When saying Nabokov's otherworld concern, Alexandrov notices that "Nabokov's textual patterns and intrusions into his fictional texts emerge as imitations of the otherworld's formative role with regard to man and nature" (*Nabokov's Otherworld* 18). The joy and bliss experienced by both the artist who creates a pattern imitating nature and the reader who discovers the artist's laying out of an otherworld pattern upon the art of this world then are no less than the joy that is experienced by God the Creator.

Pinned in a literary space with a unique treatment of the "real" and a conscious implementation of otherworld sensibility, Sebastian Knight appears exceptionally flashy and his personal life and character as a man and a writer are uncertain and insubstantial. We need to consider this unreliability from two aspects: first, things about Sebastian are told by the narrator and other characters. These details then are tinged with the subjective reconstructions of them. Further, some other details of him are visualized and imagined by the narrator who quotes a considerable bunch of passages from the fictions Sebastian himself had composed. They are then the narrator V. 's personal creations. For this, Nabokov seems to agree with Proust's treatment of the characters when he interprets Proust in his *Lectures on Literature* that "a character, a personality, is never known as an absolute but always as a comparative one" (*LL* 217). Nabokov further explains that Proust, instead of chopping the character up, shows it as it exists through the notions about it of other characters so as to combine them into an artistic reality after having given a series of these prisms and shadows (*LL* 217). Second, Sebastian himself seems to have inherited from his mother and father a capricious mood and a whimsical life style, a way of living that cannot be fully understood by V. 's mother, V. himself and other characters in the novel. Sebastian's solitude, his unpopularity at school, his weird behavior at social occasions, his secret love affairs and his view points concerning literary writing and literary conventions all seem to be different from the common-sense, the convention and the mundane. Compared with this uncertainty and restlessness of Sebastian, V. seems to lead a safe, down-to-earth businessman's life, doing everything according to the routine. It is hard for V. himself to understand his father's sacrificing of his life and his happy marriage with V's mother simply for a former wife who is so restless and "light-hearted" as to abandon the family. With this contrast, we seem to find this half-brother of V. —Sebastian as the evasive double of the narrator, a double with an otherworld sensibility but painfully pinned midst the mundane people—lovers, mistresses and relatives, a double that even V. himself has no sure idea to grapple with.

Even with so many differences, V. finds sharing many traits and tastes with

Sebastian, being more and more dragged to an uncontrollable desire to know who this Sebastian really is like, what his inner working of mind is and which woman is the one that has enchanted his heart but finally ruined him. Through his intuition and artistic imagination, he creatively reads Sebastian's books and letters as a reader and re-reader that Nabokov has more or less affirmed: The reader should use "impersonal imagination and artistic delight" (*LL* 4) as authentic instrument to establish "an artistic harmonious balance between the reader's mind and the author's mind" (ibid. 4). Besides, "the good readers ought to remain a little aloof and take pleasure in this aloofness while at the same time⋯ keenly enjoy [ing] with tears and shivers—the inner weave of a given masterpiece" (*LL* 4). With this balance between the reader's mind and the author's mind, V. even comes to realize near the end of the book that Sebastian's last book is Sebastian himself and "the book is heaving and dying" like the dying man (*RLSK* 179). As a good reader with imagination and eye for delight, V. seems to have received the dead man's message near the end of the book. In constructing and resurrecting the dead half-brother's real life, V. lifts himself up from the mundane and consciously and unconsciously starts to think the way that his biographee is thinking. V. , as if being guided by his half-brother's spirit, turns to see life not from this side, but from the other side. He realizes that there is no real life story of anybody, only the infinitely near versions but infinitely unapproachable and incomplete versions. What is real is the book that is not true but plausible and he experiences the delight and bliss from his own imagination and artistic creation and as a result, so does the reader.

　　Nabokov writes of a biographer who tries to write the real life of his half-brother and finds that it is impossible to obtain his half-brother's "real" life. And it eventually dawns on the biographer that the fictional book he is writing turns out to be the truest of all. That is, the book *The Real Life of Sebastian Life* with all its extrapolations, guesses, visions and imaginations is the only "true" (plausible) thing in the world. In this story-in-story narrative framework, the living story-teller tends to merge with his dead character and the living is uncannily guided by a promise of a deliverance of an important message of the dead that is never kept but is transcendentally recreated by the story-teller in the very process of creating the story. In this involved framework, Nabokov characterizes a character that forever pushes himself to a terra incognita where the other side of the boundary between life and death is seen. This character is just like a person who is seeing the traveler off can stay late enough on the deck while not being a traveler himself. Therefore, V. is that person, a literary ruse whom Nabokov sends to see off a half-brother—Sebastian who is on board the ship to the other side of the shore to catch at least a glimpse of the otherworld. This quest for the higher consciousness of the otherworld which is hidden behind all the ordinary details and trifles in an artistic work pays tribute to an invisible hand that exerts its power on all the creatures in Nature.

To emphasize this transcendental power, Nabokov, who believes in the power of the author as the power of God the creator, imitates the mimicry in nature and creates deception through concealment in a most involved way, a way that is well beyond practical utilitarianism, simply for the delight of aesthetics. For Nabokov, "all art is deception and so is nature; all is deception in that good cheat, from the insect that mimics a leaf to the popular enticements of procreation" (*SO* 11). The epiphany that is obtained by V. is also Nabokov's idea that the bliss and delight derived from the artistic creation—creation that is not true, but plausible, are imitating the mimicry in nature. Like the invisible hand in nature that shapes and arranges things in a mysterious way, V. is following that fateful life of him to write not without the guidance of the dead and the self-conscious intrusion of the author. Designing multiple narrative levels, Nabokov magically makes his narrator trans-cross the boundaries of different ontological existences while juxtaposing one with the other through hard-to-discover signs and images. In this multi-layered artistic world, Nabokov exerts his power of author as a God to project mission upon his narrator and his double so as to reach the otherworld consciousness for the possible and positive resurrection of the dead. With his creative will to happiness, Nabokov creates his own literary kingdom where he hopes to offer an alternative to look at this world from the other side of the boundary between life and death.

I　The Real and the "Real" / Imaginative

Nabokov's literary world is a very subjective and self-conscious one. It is subjective in that the things that Nabokov selects and develops in his fictions carry with them his own personal attitude and idiocratic taste and the people in his novels are always used to express his unique understandings of the world. He firmly indicates in his discursive writings that the writers of the fictions give in their works the reality that is not the objective reality, but the "real" that is perceived by a subjective mind. There is no reality that can be fully and validly grasped. "You never get near enough because reality is an infinite succession of steps, levels of perception, false bottoms, and hence unquenchable, unattainable. You can know more and more about one thing but you can never know everything about one thing: it's hopeless" (*SO* 11). He has doubts on the absolute knowledge. This is connected with his doubts on the literature of ideas that give sweeping generalities, empty and with no feelings of the individuals. "Literature consists of such trifles. Literature consists, in fact, not of general ideas but of particular revelations, not of schools of thought but of individuals of genius. Literature is not about something: it is the thing itself" (*LL* 116). Nabokov's concern of the subjective revelation of the individuals in the literary works makes him select the details with a conscious contrivance that in turn aims at the particular revelation. His works are self-conscious in that he believes in the power of the author as God. In his *Lectures on Literature*, he affirms Flaubert's ideal of a writer of fiction: " [He is] like God in His world, so the author in his book should be nowhere and everywhere, invisible and omnipresent" (97). Nabokov manipulates the material in such a conscious way so as to assert a position/an identity that is free from the confinement of the time and space and thus pushes the consciousness of the author/character to the fore.

The breaking of the time-and-space confinement is achieved by the artistic recombination of the past and the present and this reinforces the subjective aspect of the "real" . Nabokov once heavily quoted Marcel Proust's understanding of reality that he also documents to facilitate his own analysis of Proust's book:

What we call reality is a certain relationship between sensations and memories which surround us at the same time, the only true relationship, which the writer must recapture so that he may for ever link together in his phrase its two distinct elements. One may list in an interminable description the objects that figured in the place described, but truth will only begin when the writer takes two different objects, establishes their relationship, and encloses them in the necessary rings of his style (art) , or even when, like life itself, comparing similar qualities in two sensations, he makes their essential nature stand out clearly by joining them in a metaphor in order to remove them from the contingencies (the accidents) of time, and links them together by means of timeless words. (*LL* 211)

When Nabokov discusses the epiphany experienced by the narrator in Proust's *Swann's Way* in his *Lectures on Literature*, he says that "the narrator received three revelations—the combined sensations of the present and recollections of the past—the uneven cobbles, the tingles of a spoon, the stiffness of a napkin" (222). Then he says "for the first time he [the narrator] realizes the artistic importance of this experience" (222). The sensations of the present and the recollections of the past are what Proust refers to the two objects that should be connected by the timeless words—the words of artistic creation and only by doing this can the truth be reached. In this segment of analysis, Nabokov emphasizes the relationship between the past and the object while indicating clearly what the "reality" he believes is: it is a labor in vain to recapture the past because the past is hidden somewhere outside the realm, beyond the reach of intellect, in some material object or in the sensation which the material object will give us. And as for that object, it depends on chance whether we come upon it or not before we ourselves must die. (*LL* 222) For Nabokov, only when the object in the past has the chance of being resurrected in the present sensation by a creative consciousness with imagination can the "real" be expressed and thus the revelation is achieved.

The chance of the past memories/objects being resurrected relies in a way on the active and responsive consciousness. A consciousness can artificially and imaginatively establish connections between the things. This artifice that the artist has put into his work is made an analogy to nature as is indicated by Proust and is quoted by Nabokov in *Lectures on Literature*:

> From this point of view regarding the true way of art, was not nature herself a beginning of art, she who had often allowed me to know the beauty of something only a long time afterwards and only through something else—midday at Combray through the remembered sound of its bells and the taste of its flowers. (*LL* 211)

Proust makes an analogy between art and nature for the reason that both contain artifice and self-consciousness and both can give people revelation afterwards through a sensitive and imaginative mind. Nabokov goes further and makes "nature" and "artifice" into synonyms to stress that there is a higher consciousness in "nature" and "artifice". This invisible power can be seen in the coincidences of the details discovered by the careful readers from Nabokov's works. The coincidences can be considered in two different ways: one is that they are "a literary model of fate"; the other is that they are "the author's underscoring the artificiality of his text" (Alexandrov, *The Garland Companion* 553). While the former says of the naturalness in the coincidences of the details, the latter is about the unnaturalness in the ways of the construction of the details. Nabokov's characteristic practice of letting the author intrude upon the texts emphasizes the latter's understanding of the coincidences of details, implying that patterns and coincidences, not occurring in the real life and denying the texts' verisimilitude, are managed by the author artificially for aesthetic delight. Nabokov insists that "the entire world of nature is also filled with patterning that implies it was fashioned by some higher consciousness and all is the product of ingenious and non-utilitarian and deceptive craftsmanship" (ibid. 554). When the unnatural is called to attention, art, as what Nabokov says, "is a divine game…because this is the element in which man comes nearest to God through becoming the true creator in his own right" (*LRL* 106). Therefore, Nabokov's art in a way inherits the Romantic idea that "the artist is

God's rival and that man's artistic creations are analogues to God's natural world" (ibid. 555). Like what Friedrich Ast says, "Artistic production and divine production are one and God is revealed in the poet as he produces corporally in the visible universe" (ibid. 555).

But because of the intrusion of the author through Romantic irony in his art, Nabokov's art is modern and self-conscious, different from the relatively shapeless and eclectic aesthetic of " organic form " in German Romanticism. Further, Nabokov's art seems unnatural and "artificial" in comparison with the "reality" in the late nineteenth century and twentieth century literary works. The sui generis understanding of reality as represented in art and the authorial intrusion upon the text make Nabokov's art different from any other literary schools: 1) His work has strong romantic sensibilities, but his romantic irony refuses to endorse any passive acceptance of the romantic conventions. 2) His self-conscious construction of a literary realm denies the verisimilitude of the "reality" in the works and his laying bare the writing devices puts him into post-modern artists who doubt on the traditional realistic depiction of the world and who are good at writing metafiction. But unlike those post-modern writers, he has strong faith in the power of the author as God, who, far from being dead, can manipulate in a way that transcends time and space. As a result, the author's concern of an eternity and happiness in otherworld cannot be accepted by the post-modernist who denies any divine transcendence. 3) Like the naturalist, he is critical and exact in details, but unlike them who use the details solely to underscore the social reality for social reforms and political ideologies, he has his details to sustain the past memories that have been evoked by the present sensations. 4) He is sensitive to words and enjoys greatly the delight brought by the sounds of various verbal combinations. But instead of being a writer of versification, he aims to make the words and his otherworld thoughts unit with each other so that they can meet in the other side of the shore.

With his unique understanding of the "real", the imagination (the imagination that joins the past memory and the present sensation together) and "natural artifice," we can summarize Nabokov's art of the "real" and imagination into the following aspects: 1) Nabokov's detailed description of the "real" things in the novel is the combination of the past memories and the present sensations. It is the artistic imagination that transcends the past and the present to make both the writer and the reader experience the important artistic delight. 2) In the "real" settings, Nabokov consciously scatters the details in association with each other through different devices to hint at the fateful power of life and art. This textual pattern lying beneath the superficially unrelated details indicates that there is some higher consciousness present in it. 3) Nabokov's intrusion upon the texts, though in an indirect way through characters in *The Real Life of Sebastian Knight*, hints at the existence of the otherworld spirit and it is this otherworld concern that enables the characters to obtain revelations and consciously constructs a happy life meaningful and positive to live in. 4) By joining the real objects with imagination, the real in traditional texts becomes the Nabokovian "real" and the present is thus connected with the past memories through artistic evocation and imagination. In this context of the "real" and imagination, authorial artifice is brought to the limelight and Nabokov's art is seen imitating the mimicry of nature, aiming at the aesthetic non-utilitarianism that Nature has created simply for the delight of the eye.

The Real Life of Sebastian Knight provides a sufficient framework for Nabokov's the "real" and imagination since the whole book is concerned with the objects and people of the past and the revocation of them through information collection, present sensation, subjective selection, construction and visualization. In this sense, this work can be seen as the joining of the two "objects" of the past and present through the narrator—V. ; his effort in the writing of a biography of his half-brother Sebastian is the joining of his and the other characters' past memories and his present sensations that are obtained from collecting the past information. The particular understanding of the "real" by V in the novel is set against the reality understood in a conventional sense in the first page of the book. The narrator told of an elderly Russian lady who gave V the diary she had kept in the past. According to V. , the diary turns out to be dry: "So uneventful had those years been (apparently) that the collecting of daily details···barely surpassed a short description of the day's weather; and it is curious to note in this respect that the personal diaries of sovereigns—no matter what troubles beset their realms—are mainly concerned with the same subject" (*RLSK* 5). Then with the lady's diary, V. can describe the weather of the morning of Sebastian's birth: "a fine windless one, with twelve degrees below zero···" (*RLSK* 5) But being aware that it is insufficient to give the reader "the implied delights of a winter day···in St. Petersburg, V. in the next passage gives what he considers to be the "real" winter day in Petersburg:

> The pure luxury of a cloudless sky designed not to warm the flesh, but solely to please the eye; the sheen of sledge-cuts on the hard-beaten snow of spacious streets with a tawny tinge about the middle tracks due to a rich mixture of horse-dung; the brightly colored bunch of toy-balloons hawked by an aproned pedlar; the soft curve of a cupola, its gold dimmed by the bloom of powdery frost; the birch trees in the public gardens, every tiniest twig outlined in white; the rasp and tinkle of winter traffic. (*RLSK* 5—6)

This description of the winter scene in St. Petersburg later is explained as evoked by the old postcard that is placed on his desk to keep the child of memory amused. It involves three aspects.

First, it is the objects themselves. The sky, the snow on the street, the toy-balloons, the cupola, the trees, their twigs and the moving traffic all combine to form a three-dimensional picture with the objects ranging from sky to mid-air to earth. These objects are all associated with each other by the snow— the significant sign of a Russian winter day. In the sensually and meticulously constructed verbal pictorial world of Russian winter, the real objects that one can find in any realistic novel are all filtered through someone's five senses, perceived with a strong focus on the impressions made on an extremely responsive consciousness whose tentacles are all open. Second, it is the memory of the past. These objects subjectively perceived contain the past memories of V. —his memories of a particular Russian winter day when he himself was in there. These past memories are evoked by the old picture postcard that he has placed on his desk to "keep the child of memory amused" (*RLSK* 6). With a distance in time and space, V, who is now at his 18th year of life in exile in Paris, recalls this scenery out of the request of describing the morning of Sebastian's birth—the writing of the book to be specific. According to Nabo kov, when he comments on Proust's work, a work of art is our only means of thus capturing the past and the recreating of impressions through the memory is almost the very essence of a work of art. (*LL* 249) With this help of the past memory, the objects are no longer real, becoming "real" in Nabokovian sense with artistic evocations in it. Third, it is the revelation on the part of the person who recalls. V. , after writing down the above quotation of his recalled past of Russian winter day, says:

> By the way how queer it is when you look at an old picture postcard…to consider the haphazard way Russian cabs had of turning whenever they liked, anywhere and anyhow, so that instead of the straight, self-conscious stream of modern traffic one sees—on this paint-ed photograph—a dream-wide street with droshkies all awry under in-credibly blue skies…melt automatically into a pink flush of mnemonic banality. (*RLSK* 6)

In this quoted passage, V. 's extended ramifications on the past memories when being compared with the present here and now overwhelm him with a queer feeling and lead him to the mnemonic banality that now has become a dream-like world. With the recalling, the past and the present are combined, vying for dominance. In the second quoted passage, V. , with the help of the depiction of the past winter day in Russia, comes to an active revelation achieved through comparison of the past and the present. In this way, he realized what Nabokov comments on the evocation of the past in interpreting Proust's works: "If we can retain the sense of our own identity, and at the same time live fully in that mo-ment which we had for long believed to be no more, then, and only then, we are at last in full possession of lost time" (*LL* 249).

Putting the mnemonic "real" along side with the unimaginative reality that is common in the traditional literary canon, Nabokov forces the reader to compare and contrast the two modes of realities in literature: one is the details presented as if they are seen through a bland glass, transparent, matter-of-fact and straightforward, leaving no room for one's thoughts and imagination to play. As the backdrop of the novel echoing more or less the development of the plot and characterization, this kind of presentation of the reality is constructed for the verisimilitude of the reality so as to make believe that the fictional "real" is what exactly happens in real life. The other mode is to give the details of the world as if they are filtered and examined through the colorful glasses under sunlight, reflecting a real world that has been transformed and reconstructed by a consciousness, a consciousness that infuses the objects in the real world with his past memories and present sensations, thus transcending time and space, eternally recreating the lost things found through art. V. 's ramifications on his past experiences on Russian winter day and his evocation of his sensations on the first two pages of the book set the tone for the whole novel: his recalling of the past life of his dead half-brother relies heavily on this kind of emotional, fictional and sensual reconstructions of the past rather than on the way his biographee "walked, or laughed or sneezed···" because "all this [the latter] would be no more than sundry bits of cinema-film cut away by scissors and having nothing in common with the essential drama. " (*RLSK* 18) Being affirmed that in Sebastian's life "drama there was" (*RLSK* 18), V. resorts to the mode of the "real" to excavate the drama in Sebastian's life by quoting Sebastian's most autobiographical book: *Lost Property*, a book which intrinsically echoes Nabokov's treatment of the "real" .

In *Lost Property*, Sebastian writes that "my discovery of England put new life into my most intimate memories. " (*RLSK* 18) What he refers to the discovery literally is his finding a place called Roquebrune where his mother died thirteen years ago. There in a pension his mother lived, Sebastian, sitting in the garden, "tried to see the pink house and the tree and the whole complexion of the place as my mother had seen it. " (*RLSK* 19) Though not knowing which room his mother lived, he constructs an image of a bed of purple pansies in front of his eyes as if his mother, once sitting there, viewed the same view. The result is:

Gradually I worked myself into such a state that for a moment the pink and green seemed to shimmer and float as if seen through a veil of mist. My mother, a dim slight figure in a large hat, went slowly up the steps which seemed to dissolve into water. A terrific thump made me regain consciousness. An orange had rolled down out of the paper bag on my lap···Some months later in London I happened to meet a cousin of hers. A turn of conversation led me to mention that I had visited the place where she had died. 'oh,' he said, 'but it was the other Roquebrune, the one in the Var.' (*RLSK* 19—20)

Assuming this pension as the one his mother lived before her death and judging by the villa's name "Les Violettes," Sebastian invents a bed of purple pansies and also tries to see the whole place in his dead mother's eyes. Through his keen eagerness for the communion with her and his love for her, Sebastian seems to go back to the past when his mother was still alive. The bed of purple pansies and his love combine to transport him from the real surroundings to the otherworld where the spirit of the dead is evoked and reveals itself. Sebastian's mental efforts and his unique imaginative power help him to shrug off the earthly confinements and enter a space where the living and the dead have no boundary between each other. But, as we know, the place where he evoked his mother's soul is the wrong pension with an identical name and the right one is the one in the Var. After knowing this truth, Sebastian, as what he says, had a discovery that adds new life to his most intimate memories: the real surroundings are not important. It is the imaginative power of one's creation that evokes the soul and thus enjoys the unearthly bliss.

V. also seems to affirm this since he says that Sebastian's secretary—Mr. Goodman in his biography of Sebastian—*The Tragedy of Sebastian Knight* misses the real intention of the writer and quotes the same passage for another unimaginative theme: "Sebastian Knight was so enamored of the burlesque side of things and so incapable of caring for their serious core that he managed···to make fun of intimate emotions, rightly held sacred by the rest of humanity" (*RLSK* 20). Mr. Goodman is not only a second-class writer who writes his biography of Sebastian with commonsense judgments and self-satisfied ideas but a bad reader who is trapped by deception, irony and superficial meanings deliberately set by the ingenious writer, thus missing the hidden meanings of the text. Reading literature as political or social documents, Mr. Goodman literally interprets Sebastian's love of his mother through artistic construction of the soul of the beloved as burlesque. And his concern with the real fact—the fact that the pension where Sebastian evokes creatively the image of his mother is not the right place betrays Goodman's mediocre taste in art and his lack of understanding of what true art is. Being trapped, Goodman can only jump into the judgment: Sebastian is making fun of the most sacred emotions that other people cherish.

Judging Sebastian's work through the conventional understanding of reality in literature, Mr. Goodman is sure to fail to understand the true messages that Sebastian intends to design for his reader: 1) Sebastian reappropriates the romantic literature of expressing human emotions and makes it a purer one through parody. When Sebastian went to the garden of the pension, he is not expected as the reader of the romantic literature to see the things lyrical and ideal and he is not described as being overwhelmed with the luxurious feelings that we always find in such literature. Rather, he "noticed a bunch of violets clumsily painted on the gate" (*RLSK* 19). In addition, "an old man naked as far down as I could see peered at me from a balcony" (*RLSK* 19). These very unromantic scenes to appear in such a sacred moment remind us of the similar ugly scene that occurs in *Lolita* when young Humbert and his Annabel are about to make love. These juxtapositions of the emotional scenes with the vulgar ones call our attention to the difference of these two and the difference between the traditional treatment and Sebastian's treatment on the same occasion.

Acknowledging the traditional convention of romantic prose, Sebastian parodies it and gives romantic prose a new, purer form and makes it his own at the same time. But Mr. Goodman's literal reading represents the bunch of commonsense readers who expect what the traditional biography romance would offer them. 2) Sebastian is concerned with the construction of inner "real" revelation through the objects in the surroundings. It is the revelation that transports one to the otherworld that gives people a new meaning to his life. Through a will to the otherworld, one can communicate with the lost people or thing by artistic imagination. With the revelation that V. has come all the way to obtain at the end of the novel, the soul of the dead is seen to dwell anywhere so long as "you find and follow its undulations" (*RLSK* 204). This otherworld quest can never be grasped by a simple mind stuffed with generalities and only responsive to all *Poshlost* as Mr. Goodman's. 3) Art is artifice. Only when one reads with imagination and concerns with the existence of a higher consciousness hidden behind can one grasp the hidden meaning. This needs to be explained through the association of this passage with Sebastian's in his *Lost Property* with V's epiphany at the end of the book. In *The Real Life of Sebastian Knight*, V. took both a train and a taxi to go to Sebastian's deathbed to have the last meeting. But V. , like Sebastian in the above quoted passage, mistook another patient as Sebastian and got his revelation. Echoing with Sebastian, V. 's experience carries the same message with Sebastian's in the spiritual communion with the dead (When V. arrived at the hospital, Sebastian had already been dead for several hours).

In V. 's passage in the book, we can see that he actually experienced the same sensation as Sebastian had in his own life. Like Sebastian who, though mistakes his mother's pension, gets revelation all the same, V. , unknowingly looking at the wrong man, feels safe, hopeful, positive, happy and inspiring at the sight of the man who is still alive and starts to see life in a new way: "How little I knew of his life! But now I was learning something every instant. That door standing ajar was the best link imaginable. That gentle breathing was telling me more of Sebastian than I had ever known before" (*RLSK* 203). The breathing of course is not Sebastian's, but it now seems to serve as a medium for V. to transport himself to the otherworld to know what he wants to know. Like Sebastian, he now learns in an unknowing way to experience the artistic delight of creation. Also like Sebastian, by totally merging himself with Sebastian, and shrugging his bodily confinement, V. worked himself to a state that even in front of a wrong man, he got his revelation: "So I did not see Sebastian after all, or at least I did not see him alive. But those few minutes I spent listening to what I thought was his breathing changed my life as completely as it would have been changed, had Sebastian spoken to me before dying"

(*RLSK* 204).

　　We should consider these two messages (Sebastian's and V. 's) from two aspects: a) The echoing of the two passages by the two writers in different narrative levels hint at the "natural artifice" of Nabokov in his context of the "real" and imagination. Both passages involve the image of the specter such as the veil of mist and breathing of a dying man. Both involve discoveries and revelations on the metaphysical level. The two passages come at the critical moment of the character's shrugging off his life confinement and trying to merge himself with the soul of the other dying or dead person. The outside surroundings come as secondary compared with inner spiritual communication. The construction of the two passages in this way indicates Nabokov's intrusion as an artist to strike his real intention of his book—the higher consciousness hidden behind the characters in two levels of narration. b) The position of the two passages (One is in the first chapter and the other is in the last chapter) in the book well indicates the thematic meaning of this arrangement: V. 's maturation of his consciousness and his achieving of his hard-earned revelation of the existence of a higher consciousness along with the composition of this book.

II　The Life of Sebastian Knight

　　Sebastian's "real" life is the central concern of the narrator V. in the book and it is also the primary motivation for his narration. In the process of collecting the materials for his biography, V. constantly asks the question: Who is Sebastian Knight? What is really going on in his mind? What is his real life, the life that contains the real essential drama? V. 's plan of writing a biography on Sebastian and his curiosity on Sebastian's life encourage him to take the writing class, combing Sebastian's house for information, having interviews with Sebastian's friends, looking for Sebastian's secret lovers, reading and commenting on Sebastian's books as well as the critical books of them. Based on these, V. presents the life of Sebastian from his own memories, his readings of Sebastian's books, Sebastian's friends and lovers. Handled in this way, Sebastian, like a coal glimmering in the distant darkness, flashes in and out of those episodic textual fragments about him. His life, perceived and filtered by V. and other characters, seems to refuse to settle on any firm and stable ground, thus moving in the text ghostly, hiding behind, lurking in a corner, nowhere to be seen but everywhere.

Being the major narrative motivation, Sebastian does speak. He speaks through his books, his letters, and his love affairs. But there is always a point that we should not neglect: his existence is always attached to V. 's experience of traveling and hunting for information about his life stories. This attachment, being Sebastian's only connection with the mundane life, serves as a foil to make Sebastian's life that is involved around the otherworld stand out. Moving in and out of V. 's life circle, Sebastian trans-crosses the mundane life and otherworld life, showing himself alternatively in light and shadows. In V. 's eyes, those unknown parts of Sebastian are closely connected with the most intimate, secret, capricious elements, something that people in the mundane can never understand. Therefore, the more uncertainly Sebastian's mundane life is delivered, the more prominent his otherworld concern appears. To see what has been constructed by V. in terms of Sebastian's love affairs and literary production can help us to understand the textual and thematic function of this character for both V. the narrator and Nabokov the writer's sake.

Sebastian's life is narrated mainly through four periods of time: his life in Russia before exile, university years in Cambridge, his love affair with Clare Bishop and Nina—his dark love. These are not narrated in a strict chronological way and they are relayed with a lot of other incidents and digressions. Still we can follow the fragments of his life roughly from the 1st period (1910—1919), 2nd period (1920—1924), 3rd period (1924—1930, with his affair starting from 1929 with the dark lady—Nina), 4th period (1930—1936, with Mr. Goodman as his secretary from 1930—1934). From V. 's memories of childhood and youth (from 1910 to 1919) before leaving Russia, Sebastian is that kind of listless and tongue-tied person with constant aloofness, paying no attention to V.. Being cold and impatient and immersed in his poem-writing and picture-drawing in V. 's memories, Sebastian escapes both V. and V. 's mother's understanding. Going out on an adventure with a futurist couple at the age of 17 years old and talking later as a dispassionate observer, Sebastian remains a total mystery. The rare meetings with V. in Paris also do not help much. Deduced from Sebastian's book *Lost Property*, V. fills the blank of Sebastian's attitude toward his exile life and his motherland and is sure that Sebastian should be like himself: being nostalgic of his motherland, but at the same time feeling bitter at the political activities going on there. Apart from his memories and his deductions from Sebastian's life in Russia, V. also went to Cambridge to get some glimpses of Sebastian's university life. He learned that after the first year's adaptation to the new environment and the rhythm of university life, the not-so-successful Sebastian began to follow his own rhythm and "started to cultivate self-consciousness as if it had been some rare talent or passion" (*RLSK* 44). And "only then did Sebastian derive satisfaction from its rich and monstrous growth, ceasing to worry about his awkward un-congeniality" (ibid. 44).

Then in 1924, V. came across Sebastian when Sebastian was with Clare in Paris, talking of the novel that he had just finished. This period saw Sebastian as the healthiest person he had ever seen in him, in very good state, producing two novels and three stories. Being mnemogenic and imaginative, Clare fits into Sebastian's life very well:

> Clare, who had not composed a single line of imaginative prose or poetry in her life, understood so well (and that was her private miracle) every detail of Sebastian's struggle, that the words she typed were to her so much the conveyors of their natural sense, but the curves and gaps and zigzags showing Sebastian's groping along a certain ideal line of expression. (*RLSK* 84)

However, at the end of that decade, in 1929, Sebastian met a secret lady with whom he can not live without though he knows very well that she is "vain and cheap" (*RLSK* 160). He has correspondence with her in Russian. In the last six years of Sebastian's life, he drains away from his friends and V. and had several secret journeys that no one knows the destination. Through this last period, Sebastian isolated himself further away from the normal life and abandoned his regular life routine. This was the time that he kept the relationship with that secret, dark love—some woman called Nina he met in 1929. Being abandoned by her and tortured by his heart disease, he kept himself away from solitude, destroying himself by appearing in various social occasions. Even though he makes his appearances in these social occasions, his weird behaviors made him even queerer. The last and saddest year of Sebastian saw his completion of his master-piece—*The Doubtful Asphodel* whose major concern is that the hero is dying. About a week before Sebastian's death, Sebastian wrote a letter to V. , saying that he wanted to see him for some important things to say to him. Even though V. did not manage to see him before Sebastian's death, he got his own revelation of the whole thing.

Starting from the year 1927 when Sebastian suddenly was diagnosed as having the same disease with his mother (who was killed by this very disease), there were something that happened that had changed Sebastian's life and his relationship with Clare. He was beyond her, struggling for something that people around him took it as his usual fit in composing the novels. Growing more and more strange, he stopped talking to Clare at all. The reasons for that are not clearly indicated in the text, but it is sure that some other woman came into Sebastian's life and that made him restless and fidgeting. Then one cannot help wondering what V. was aiming at in questing for Sebastian's love life by going all the way from Berlin to Paris to hunt for his secret lover, the one that had destroyed Sebastian during his last years in the world. I think V. 's words can be in some way served as a guide to V. 's real intentions:

My quest had developed its own magic and logic and though I sometimes cannot help believing that it had gradually grown into a dream, that quest, using the pattern of reality for the weaving of its own fancies, I am forced to recognize that I was being led right, and that in striving to render Sebastian's life I must now follow the same rhythmical interlacements. (*RLSK* 137)

Affirming the importance of the rhythmical interlacements that exist in-between the real facts of one's life, V. resorts to Sebastian's emotional life and justifies his subjective construction of the love stories of Sebastian as the intuitive, truer version of Sebastian's life through the inner connections between them two. Thus, Sebastian's love life then becomes V. 's major issue to grope for the essential drama in Sebastian's life rather than the cinema-film cuttings of his factual life. In this passage, V. takes his writing of the biography as a quest that had grown into a dream that is using the pattern of reality for the weaving of its own fancies. Clearly, the quest for the details of Sebastian's life has become for V. a weaving for his own fancies under the cover of the quest for the realities of Sebastian's life. It is the wave and trembling beneath the superficial facts of Sebastian's life that V. is questing.

Following "some kind of rhythm" (*RLSK* 34) that is supposed by him as shared between the brothers, V. uses the reality of Sebastian's life as a ruse, a skeleton, or a structural device to weave the fanciful life of Sebastian along with V. the writer's own imaginative constructions. Thus, making these clear, V. moves to demonstrate his own artifice in weaving Sebastian's emotional life:

> There seems to have been a law of some strange harmony in the placing of a meeting relating to Sebastian's first adolescent romance in such close proximity to the echoes of his last dark love. Two modes of his life question each other and the answer is his life itself, and that is the nearest one ever can approach a human truth. (*RLSK* 137)

That Sebastian's first love and the last dark love meet together is obviously the result of the artificiality of V. 's construction. His imaginative recreation and recombination of Sebastian's emotional life, consciously and unconsciously, makes him realize that this is what really constitutes Sebastian's life. From the perspective of V. the writer, the two modes of life of Sebastian refer to the real facts and the recreation of these facts that are flavored with subjective fancies. From Sebastian's perspective, these two modes of life refer to his conscious moves of emotion that he can control and those unconscious ones that seem to be arranged by fate, by some higher consciousness and he is forced to follow. To be specific: 1) they refer to the mundane, positive love that the normal person experiences and the love that is so negatively passionate and unbearable that it may turn a person's life topsy-turvy. 2) These two modes for V. the biographer are respectively the love that he, as a half-brother, can quest, collect information about, and feel and the love that he can only depend on his visional reconstructions and some common rhythm shared by both the brothers. 3) With the above understandings, V.'s two modes come very close to the mundane love and the otherworld love; one follows the routine while the other follows instinct and fate and can never be located and explained.

Adding much fuel to the life of Sebastian, the love affairs of Sebastian are complemented by V.'s quotations of and comments on Sebastian's profuse literary works produced in each of his life stages. Reading as a creative reader, V. selects the passages from different books written by Sebastian and weaves them into his own text to complement the life of his biographee. To justify his quotations and comments, V. remarks:

> He [Sebastian] had a queer habit of endowing even his most grotesque characters with this or that idea, or impression, or desire which he himself might have toyed with ··· But I fail to name any other author who made use of his art in such a baffling manner—baffling to me who might desire to see the real man behind the author ··· The light of personal truth is hard to perceive in the shimmer of an imaginary nature, but what is still harder to understand is the amazing fact that a man writing of things which he really felt at the time of writing, could have the power to create simultaneously ··· a fictitious and faintly absurd character. (*RLSK* 114)

In this passage, V. is transferring two levels of meanings. As any reasonable enough reader, V., out of the pure desire of hunting for the life of Sebastian, wants to find out the real man behind the author of the books. The fact is that there is something that reflects the author's true facts of life though they are hidden behind the shimmer of fictionalities of the book in Sebastian's case. But the reader should not stop at that because Sebastian the author has the power of weaving his personal issues in a highly creative way into his texts. To understand fully his art, according to V., the reader needs to have the eye and imagination to see and appreciate the recombination and recreation of the life facts of the author.

Starting from Sebastian's *The Prismatic Bezel*, *Success* to *Lost Property*, *Doubtful Asphodel*, V. quotes, comments and in this process starts to see them maturing from the formation of a sui generis literary style to the formation of the unique metaphysical understanding of the otherworld on the part of Sebastian. In *The Prismatic Bezel*, Sebastian "used parody as a kind of springboard for leaping into the highest region of serious emotion" (*RLSK* 91). By using parody, Sebastian infiltrates new life into the old worn-out things, "hunting out the things which had once been fresh and bright but which were now worn to a thread, dead things among living ones; dead things shamming life, painted and repainted, continuing to be accepted by lazy minds serenely unaware of the fraud" (*RLSK* 91). Opening new ways for the reader to see the world in their own unique, imaginative way, Sebastian at the same time shows great contempt to whatever thing that is "second-rate, not the third or N-th rate because here, at the readable stage, the shamming began, and this was, in an *artistic* sense, immoral" (*RLSK* 92).

Confirming this as the most humane and moral way of rendering life and art in literary works, V. proceeds to introduce Sebastian's second novel as concerning with the human fate in *Success*. "Rising a step further", according to V., Sebastian in his second novel goes beyond the mere literary stylistic devices. His intrusion as an author and his controlling of the details about the characters and events as his literary artifice make the fateful meetings of the man and the woman unavoidable. This brings out his important idea that something of a higher consciousness is working behind in the dark in his understanding of both life and art. The reason for saying so is based on the last chapter Sebastian wrote in *Success* where, according to V., "contains a passage so strangely connected with Sebastian's inner life⋯that it deserves being quoted" (*RLSK* 98). In it, the hero William, struggling for the understanding of his matter-of-fact and mundane fiancé who is impossible to share with him the otherworld sensibility, desperately chooses to end the relationship. This episode is read by V. as Sebastian's true love affairs with his lovers. Inheriting the capriciousness and restlessness of his late mother, Sebastian is unpredictable to the mundane mind in love affairs and seems doomed to seek for some dark love that is unknown and beyond the common human beings.

Sebastian's cold treatment towards Clare bishop resulted in her departure in 1929 when Sebastian started writing his most autobiographical novel *Lost Property*. This was also the time when he developed a relationship with his dark love— Nina whom he met in Blauberg in 1927. As a turning-point in his life and art, *Lost Property* was commented by V. as "a kind of halt in his literary journey of discovery: a summing up, a counting of the things and souls lost on the way, a setting of bearings; the clinking sound of unsaddled horses browsing in the dark; the glow of a campfire; stars overhead" (*RLSK* 111). The remodeling and recombination of Sebastian's life facts and artistic construction in this autobiography provide a chance for both Sebastian and V. to have a glimpse at the selfest of his own self. In the book, Sebastian expressed his pain and pleasure in dealing with the life in the mundane and the imagination for the otherworld: "Most people live through the day with this or that part of their mind in a happy state of somnolence…but in my case all the shutters and lids and doors of the mind would be open at once at all times of the day…This state of constant wakefulness was extremely painful…" (*RLSK* 67) Therefore,

every ordinary act I [Sebastian] …had to perform, took on such a complicated appearance, provoked such a multitude of associative ideas in my mind, and these associations were so tricky and obscure, so utterly useless for practical application, that I would either shirk the business at hand or else make a mess of it out of sheer nervousness. (*RLSK* 67)

For Sebastian who knew "the dangerous vagrancies" of his consciousness, he in *Lost Property* said that he had to avoid meeting people, of hurting their feelings or making myself [Sebastian] ridiculous in their eyes" (*RLSK* 68). But this painful state in the practical side of life (the loss of his very consciousness) in Sebastian's book is said to become "an instrument of exquisite pleasure when-ever I [Sebastian] yielded to my loneliness" (*RLSK* 68).

Starting from following his own rhythm of consciousness in university years and establishing his unique way of expressing his ideas in literary works, Se-bastian now in *Lost Property* reached a state where the loss of his own con-sciousness allows him the freedom of savoring the otherworld bliss that the con-sciousness-confined state can not offer. Abandoning everything normal in com-mon people's eyes—the normal and happy love with Clare, Sebastian resorts to that state where he can see his lover in the mist even though he is "desperately unhappy" with the other woman, as that is betrayed by a love letter in *Lost Property*. What he experienced there in the relationship with the dark lady—Ni-na was not clearly told. But his last book—*The Doubtful Asphodel*, his best work, was written about that time. In that book, the hero is nearest to the oth-erworld truth. And Sebastian's concern on the otherworld truth seemed to coin-cide with his quest for his true love. Abandoning one by one his lovers who cannot share his understanding of the world, Sebastian met Nina, the capri-cious and restless lady who was cruel to refuse to see him when she could not bear him any more. Sebastian cannot live without her but at the same time knows very well that she, is like his other lovers, can not fit into his life. Being vain and cheap, Nina haunted his life and tortured Sebastian by de-stroying all his contact with the mundane world such as seeing friends, manag-ing his everyday business of seeing the publishers. This disastrous love affair drove Sebastian into a desperate person and, as a result, he experienced sev-eral death rehearsals brought by heart attack.

Being refused, Sebastian in his *The Doubtful Asphodel* abandoned his con-sciousness and seemed to have entered into a state where the consciousness is cast off, just as the dying hero in the book. Through the character's mouth, Se-bastian uttered his understandings about the truth that only when one is about to die can see:

The hardest knot is but a meandering string; tough to the finger nails,
but really a matter of lazy and graceful loopings. The eye undoes it, while

clumsy fingers bleed. He (the dying man) was that knot, and he would be untied at once, if he could manage to see and follow the thread. And···everything would be unraveled, —everything that he might imagine in our childish terms of space and time, both being riddles invented by man as riddles, and thus coming back at us: the boomerangs of nonsense···Now he had caught something real, which had nothing to do with any of the thoughts or feelings, or experiences he might have had in the kindergarten of life···" (*RLSK* 178)

This spiritual revelation breaks the confinement of time and space, the mundane and the physical, reaching the other side of the boundary between life and death. The attempt to reach the otherworld truth coincided with the last attempt to maintain the relationship with Nina: "The appearance of *The Doubtful Asphodel* in the spring of 1935 coincided with Sebastian's last attempt to see Nina" (*RLSK* 183). V. 's remarks seem to hint that the books produced by Sebastian are the breath of his life, the rhythm of his love, the heaving in and out of the air in the lung. Far from being cold and making fun of the serious emotions of human being as what Mr. Goodman had wrongly criticized, Sebastian is showing the most humane emotions in a most unique way. Rehearsing death both in a literal and figurative (artistic) way, Sebastian weaved his emotional experience and imaginative version of his life facts into his book, offering the reader his hard-gained revelation out of the fire of life.

Tracing the love life and literary discoveries of Sebastian, we see that there is a clear recognition of his consciousness in responding to the world outside and summing up of his discoveries. His childhood and his youth before leaving Russia are sketched in some patches of V. 's memories, rendered in a distant mist, reconstructed by V. as some external impressions roughly left on the mind of a child 6 years younger than Sebastian. Though Sebastian's book is quoted to help illustrate his understanding of his motherland and the events happened around him, Sebastian is obviously reluctant to openly and directly talk about the social and political events. Even in his *Lost Property* that is quoted by V. , he is seen shunning away from any sentimental pouring of feelings on his homeland: "because the theme [the love of the banished man toward his country] has already been treated by my betters and also because I have an innate distrust of what I feel easy to express, no sentimental wanderer will ever be allowed to land on the rock of my unfriendly prose" (*RLSK* 27). Sebastian's secret tour with the futurist couple also proved to be a necessary test in his understanding of the social affairs. But the fact that the beliefs and ideas of the couple later turned out to be a comedy and a farce was well seen by Sebastian as an inalienable part of the painted world of sham.

Refusing anything ready-made, trite and widely-accepted, Sebastian in his university life gradually cast off the accepted university rules and followed his own rhythm. The formation and realization of his unique consciousness went along with his novel writing and love affairs. Following more and more his inner trembling, Sebastian was more steeped into his artistic world, staying aloof and weird in his friends and lovers' eyes. Straining away from the outside mundane world, Sebastian perceives more clearly that he is doomed to live another life, a life in which he feels free and creative and he can immerse himself in the bliss that no other things can bring to him. Demonstrating his discoveries in his literary works, Sebastian gives his books the very living breath he is panting in and out. His life and art are coincident with each other with the same tempo, especially when he met the capricious and changeable Nina. Being doomed to be deeply attached to a love affair that he knows very well wrong and absurd, Sebastian makes a mess of his mundane life but turns to seek to the other side of life in his novel to reach even further the ultimate state of human being. Casting off layer by layer the mundane concerns, Sebastian moves toward his fateful direction of his spiritual revelation and finished his masterpiece which records his last years of life and discoveries. *The Doubtful Asphodel* provides Sebastian a literary space for him to exert his power on the materials and characters in his novel, achieving the artistic freedom in a full sense. His unique verbal expressions that Sebastian had developed in his early literary works are now seen as the means to embody and carry out his unique intellectual ideas. When the words and thoughts are combined as one and when the mundane life fragments and creative imagination interlace with each other, the books of Sebastian best summarize his life and art.

Thus said, Sebastian's life in both its literal and figurative sense constitutes the ultimate force of narration for V.. Knowing very well the life facts of Sebastian are not the things that can render the essential drama of his inner life, V. gradually uses the reality of Sebastian's life as his ruse to demonstrate both Sebastian's inner conflicts and tensions and his revelations. Through the reconstruction of the information collected on Sebastian and his creative interpretations of Sebastian's artistic works, V. comes to perceive through the soul and sensibility of Sebastian his own life and value. As a writing narrator, a character and a reader, V. seems to tell us through his three-fold roles how to write a biography—the real life of Sebastian, how to interpret Sebastian's artistic works and how to achieve one's revelation through Sebastian's life and art. V. 's warnings on reading and writing and distilling revelations can be seen in various places in the book. His conscious moves and instructions in the writing of a biography of Sebastian betray Nabokov's concern and ideas. First of all, the distant relationship of Sebastian and V. reflects Nabokov's behavior toward his younger brother Sergey. Second, Sebastian shares many other traits with Nabokov. They were both born in 1899 and fled to the continent from Russia as a result of revolution. They both attended Cambridge University and wrote very unique literary works in English and both had a special feeling for Russian language that they both excelled much better than their English. The duel that killed his father in the book is also based on Nabokov's father's life. And the love affair of Sebastian with that dark lady also reflects Nabokov's extramarital love affair with Irina Guadanini.

To express his literary ideas on writing, reading, and otherworld concern, Nabokov invents an involved world of art in which the narrator attempts to represent its fictional character's life through the character's life, love and fictional works. He is impersonal in his art, inventing V. to write the real life of Sebastian. But at the same time, he is personal in infusing his own consciousness in Sebastian's life events. Nabokov's personal concerns, when being recreated by his impersonal art, make it hard for the reader not to contemplate his intensions through combining the two worlds of his artistic construction: the "real" that he derived from the combination of the past memories and the present sensation and the imaginative that he weaves into his "real" . For V. , Sebastian's life and art offer him a chance to reside in Sebastian's soul and thus achieve his own revelation through visualizing Sebastian's quest for otherworld. For Nabokov, V. 's revelation obtained from the writing of the book serves as Nabokov's mouthpiece to air out his literary quest and concerns in both theme and style. It is true that *The Real Life of Sebastian Knight* is a fictional work that, though containing some ideas and sensibilities of the author, is independent from its composer once it is finished. But for an author who has strong self-conscious sensibility in constructing all the materials in God's way as Nabokov, we have very good reasons to believe that Nabokov practices his verbal artistic style and metaphysical theme in a metafictional novel that encloses another novel, in a narrator/writer that arouses another writer/narrator, in a life story that incurs another life story.

III   V. 's Epiphany Through Fictional Construction

V. in the book plays three roles: as a narrator to render the story in various discourses; as a writer concerned with the framework and materials of his biography; as a reader to interpret and process the literary works by and information on Sebastian. These three roles combine to allow V. to present the most subjective biographies possible. As a narrator, V. is a reliable narrator who uses first person narration to give the reader his understanding of his characters, his comments on the character's feelings and emotions. In his narration, V. , as a limited omnipotent narrator, asks questions, seeking for answers, confessing for his limited information and failures, explaining his every move and decision. This limitation of his omnipotent power on other characters' minds is crucial in that it offers the great chance for V. to fictionally constructs, creates and then fills the blanks of the black holes of his Biographee—Sebastian. His construction of the materials about Sebastian is therefore unavoidably subjective and impressionistic. His explanation for this is a Nabokovian warning: "don't be too certain of learning the past from the lips of the present⋯Remember that what you are told is really threefold: shaped by the teller, reshaped by the listener, concealed from both by the dead man of the tale" (*RLSK* 52). The so-called real in the book has been three times removed from the life of the dead man. What is valid now is the Nabokovian "real". In addition, the materials he uses to write Sebastian's life are meager compared with the conventional biographer and he confesses that he needs to collect information from all sides to fill in the blanks and gaps.

The most direct materials are obtained from very sketchy patches of V. 's memories and from his mother's memories. The others are obtained from the telling of Sebastian's friends and lovers. Still others are constructed by V. 's own artistic creativity. Based on these materials, V. 's narration is realized through various ways in terms of Sebastian's life: 1) He quotes Sebastian's words in direct discourse. 2) He quotes directly the words of the other characters in telling Sebastian's life. 3) He retells the stories of Sebastian learnt from the other characters in his own words. 4) He records his journey of collecting Sebastian's life and love in pure narration. 5) He speaks as if it is Sebastian who is speaking. That is, their voices, consciousnesses and souls merge with each other in free direct discourse. From the first to the fifth, V. 's power of reconstruction of Sebastian's life as a narrator is seen increasing from direct quotation from Sebastian's texts to his pure narration of his own texts concerning Sebastian's life and art. These rich layers of narrative discourses are employed according to the materials that they tend to transfer. The voices of Sebastian and other character (Nina in this case) that are delivered in their own words are quoted to talk about Sebastian's most intimate feelings and occult issues relating his life and art. The voice of Sebastian's lover Clare and his university friend, the poet and the painter are muffled and replaced by V. 's narration and retelling. For his own voice, decisions and interpretations, V. justifies them in a very reasonable way and in the last two chapters V. even tends to merge with his half-brother's breathing air to form one single voice, a voice that can talk life of Sebastian in both original and creative way.

As for V. 's physical journeys for collecting Sebastian's life information, his actual meetings with Sebastian and his arrangement of his appointments and business, we find that he uses pure narration in which he is the most authoritative agent to exert his narrative power. Even though he is not sure about some behaviors of Sebastian in his pure narration, he still finds reasons to give reasonable explanations, to make the most possible guesses and to resort to his intuition and inner rhythm shared by both him and Sebastian when he fails to glimpse at the inner thoughts of his biographee. For example, to justify his futile journey to Berlin for Sebastian's last dark lady, he said "I was not sorry that I had started off with the Berlin clue. It had at least led me to obtain an unexpected glimpse of another chapter of Sebastian's past" (*RLSK* 141). To make his decision appear reasonable, he remarks: "I knew my Paris well, so that I saw at once the most time-saving sequence in which to dispose my calls if I wanted to have done with them in one day. Let it be added, in case the reader be surprised at the rough-and-ready style of my activity, that I dislike telephoning as much as I do writing letters" (*RLSK* 142). Based on these reasons, rather than calling the people to make the matter easier, V. goes to each of them to extend his biography the way he particularly favors.

Comparing with the narrations on his physical journeys and activities taken for his quest, we can see that V uses more descriptive, emotional words and details that are apparently tinged with his artistic imaginations to play up those traditionally regarded romantic scenes that he got only second-hand. V. visualizes the life of Sebastian told by Sebastian's friends in his mental pictures, very much tinged with his own artistic constructions. Exerting his power as a narrator, V. , for example, with the information told by Natasha Rosanov, creates his visualization of the romantic scenes that Sebastian had had with the girls in Russia:

The lights go out, the curtain rises and a Russian summer landscape is disclosed···A girl is sitting at the helm, but we shall let her remain achromatic··· The picture changes: another bend of that river··· Sebastian is sitting upon the bench and reading aloud some English verse from a black copybook. . (*RLSK* 138)

These romantic scenes are depicted as if they are paintings of Sebastian's adolescent love. The past memories of Natasha are regained, made eternal and timeless, transcending the confinement of time and space through V. 's artistic combination of the past and the present. Based on the fact that these are imaginations developed through the second-hand information, V. in the pure narration combines the past memories of Natasha with his present sensations, understandings and imaginations to fill in the gaps of Sebastian's life: "As in Byron's dream, again the picture changes. It is night. The sky is alive with stars. Years later Sebastian wrote that gazing at the stars gave him a sick and squeamish feeling, as for instance when you look at the bowels of a ripped-up breast" (*RLSK* 139). Inserting his own judgments and digressions in the romantic scenes, V not only imaginatively constructs the past but also shows his and Sebastian's romantic ironies in these typical conventional episodes of intensive poignancy. In these creative pure narrations, V. shows more and more of his own capability in undertaking the writing of a "real" life of Sebastian Knight.

As for those materials concerning with Sebastian's innermost, spiritual memories and cognitions, V. resorts to direct quotations to re-present thoughts and feelings of Sebastian. In these quotations of books and letters written by Sebastian, V. gives the narrative power fully away to the character himself and tries to render the heaving breath of Sebastian. For example, early in the book when V. wants to show Sebastian's intimate feelings toward his dead mother, he quotes a long passage from *Lost Property* about Sebastian's loss of consciousness in his spiritual communication with the soul of his mother. Right after that, V. proceeds to comment on Mr. Goodman's quotation of the same passage for proving some opposite and ridiculous opinions about Sebastian. Rather than continuing to comment on Sebastian's spiritual revelation achieved at that very moment, V. turns to narrate his own particular method of writing a biography that is far different from Mr. Goodman's "biographies romancees," leaving the most important message of Sebastian' concern uncommented. The reasons for this are not very easy to be located. It might simply be Nabokov's digressional prosaic style. Or it might be V. the narrator's failure of realizing the importance of the spiritual revelations of Sebastian in his discoveries of re-evocation of the soul of the dead through artistic creativities at this stage of the book. Or he as the narrator is simply saving his own revelation till the last moment, holding up and accumulating the ever-deepening comments and interpretation of his own to his final epiphany. Whatever the reasons are, there is at least one possibility: for Nabokov's concern for an occult pattern working in both literary text and nature, V. may simply follow unconsciously a pattern that he only fully realizes later in the book. Therefore, in his quotation of Sebastian's words of his intimate memories of his mother and the resulted spiritual discovery, V. unconsciously follows a pattern that only later he fully discovers.

But unlike the part we discussed above in Chapter Two, the 18th chapter sees a great change on the part of the narrator on a similar case. In the last couple of pages, these direct quotations from Sebastian's book no longer stand on their own, filling some cognitive blanks of V. whenever the context needs. Instead, they are clustered and enveloped by V the narrator's direct comments and interpretations to influence and guide the reading of these directly quoted texts of Sebastian. Those comments and interpretations, though uttered in pure narration, sometimes share the views of Sebastian as if they are Sebastian's own interpretations of his works. Some other times V. 's digressions mean to draw particular connections between Sebastian's life and his works, aiming to derive some inspirations from Sebastian's works to enrich Sebastian's inner life. Selecting subjectively the passages from Sebastian's work and interpreting them in his own creative way, V. , through direct quotations, aims to absorb them into his own revelations and understandings of Sebastian in his discursive writings. In these contexts of direct quotation plus narrator's comments, it seems that these two different narrative discourses complement each other in that the hidden meanings in Sebastian's words unuttered are explained by V. and V. 's incapability in entering Sebastian's most intimate memories and feelings is compensated by Sebastian's words directly quoted. This combination of direct quotation of Sebastian with V. the narrator's narration reaches to such a degree in some points that the two voices merge into one, uniting to utter the words of the otherworld sensibility. There they are united in such a way that the reader tends to forget whose words are actually presented and the quotation mark has ceased to be a boundary line dividing the two.

Replacing the quoted words of Sebastian in a gradual way, V. is seen inserting more and more his own words into the passages of Sebastian. Rather than the formerly heavily quoted long bunches of passages of Sebastian without his own comments, V. in the last two chapters of the book usurps more or less Sebastian's words concerning issues of the otherworld and adopts again pure narration, exerting his role as a creator. This power and confidence in speaking out his ideas in his own words are no doubt derived from his very process of writing Sebastian's life. In the earlier part of the book, the pure narration is more used in his physical journeys and outward activities. But with the deepening of his understanding of Sebastian's world of life and art, V. seems to reside in the soul of Sebastian and can utter the words and thoughts in Sebastian's way. Gaining more confidence and creativity, V. 's pure narration has largely gone beyond the role of a traditional narrator. He has risen as a new man armed with a spiritual power and an artistic sensibility derived from the contemplation and the reading of the soul and books of the dead man and thus achieves his own revelation that no one in the mundane can ever dream of:

> The answer to all questions of life and death, 'the absolute solution' was like a traveler realizing that the wild country he surveys is not an accidental assembly of natural phenomena, but the page in a book where these mountains and forests, and fields, and rivers are disposed in such a way as to form a coherent sentence. (*RLSK* 178—179)

Realizing that the question of life and death can be answered by the artifice in nature—a prearranged fateful artifice by some invisible power behind the superficial text, V. the narrator now is transferred to be a writer who resorts to metaphors to demonstrate his idea in an artistic way. Joining the artifice both in nature and in art, V. is guided by the soul of Sebastian in the narration and finally comes to the revelation that his seemingly "accidental assembly" of episodes and fragments are actually literary artifice behind which the very soul of the dead Sebastian lies.

Fictionally constructing these materials, V. varies his narrative styles in the above mentioned five discourses, consciously inserting his role as both a narrator and a fictional writer since the five narrative discourses are all fictional except for the various degrees of fictionalities in them. V. , as a writer, in writing the life and death of Sebastian, also seems to follow intuitively some power of a pattern that lays out for him. The book V. writes seems to be scattered with various fragments, episodes, evasive stories and foreign names from a superficial reading. But like those in Sebastian's last book, they are disposed in such a way as to form a coherent sentence, an insubstantial pattern that pervades the texts of reality. With its changeable forms and fusions with the other matters and elements of the text, the pattern lurks everywhere in both nature and artistic text, hidden behind the miscellaneous camouflage, only waiting to be understood by those who have mastered its language. Following the essential drama of Sebastian's life and art rather than the external facts of life, V. immerses himself in Sebastian's world of art and seems to step into the soul of Sebastian, merging with him into one person. In addition, the meager facts that he provides make people doubt if there is this relationship with Sebastian—or it may be simply the fictional construction of V. himself in writing a biography of Sebastian to write out his own ideas.

This idea of the doubtful relationship between V. and Sebastian is proposed by some scholars such as J. B. Sisson and Alexandrov. This idea makes V. the writer more fictional in his construction of Sebastian's half-brother relationship with himself. Sisson holds that the possibility that V. may not be related to Sebastian is signaled early. According to the book *The Tragedy of Sebastian Knight* written by Mr. Goodman, Sebastian's secretary from 1930—1934, the second marriage of Sebastian's father is not mentioned at all in the book. In this case, V. says "to readers of Goodman's book I am bound to appear non-existent—a bogus relative, a garrulous imposter" (*RLSK* 6). This relationship might start from V. 's whim of attaching himself to Sebastian's fame in 1935 at the publication of Sebastian's last book, *The Doubtful Asphodel.* At that time, V. says he is struggling with a tiresome business arrangement and admits, envy of Sebastian's life: "as I sat there alone in the lugubriously comfortable hall, and read the publisher's advertisement and Sebastian's handsome black name letters, I envied his lot more acutely than I had ever envied before" (*RLSK* 180—181). Re-telling this, V.

> imagined him [Sebastian] standing in a warm cheerful room at some club, with his hands in the pockets, his ears glowing, his eyes moist and bright, a smile fluttering on his lips, —and all the other people in the room standing round him, holding glasses of port, and laughing at his jokes···It was a silly picture, but it kept shining in its trembling pattern··· as one of those colored photographs you see on the back of magazines. (*RLSK* 181)

It is not impossible that V., according to the readings of the books of Sebastian, has fictionally constructed his half-brother relationship with Sebastian. His imagination of the scenes from Sebastian's fragments of life and words from his artistic work can well allow him to write an imaginative biography of Sebastian. Though in the quotation he says that "it was a silly picture" to imagine Sebastian at some club, he still can not resist the temptation to follow the pattern shining there, a pattern that V. is attracted so much that he simply cannot brush it off.

V.'s imagination of his relationship with Sebastian might come from Sebastian's book *Lost Property* where Sebastian's narrator refers to " my small half-brother" (*RLSK* 13) in the account of his father's coming duel. This half-brother role wisely makes V. not only as an independent self but also as someone who can share the inner rhythm of Sebastian in issues and elements that he cannot possibly explore. V.'s visualization here echoes with his recount of Sebastian's plan of writing a man's biography which is not carried out actually by Sebastian. V. finds in his sorting out Sebastian's things in his flat a series of pictures of different stages of a man called Mr. H. These photos were collected by Sebastian through a newspaper announcement: " Author writing fictitious biography requires photos of gentleman···" (*RLSK* 40) Right after it, V. says he suddenly felt tired and miserable and he " wanted the face of Sebastian himself" (*RLSK* 41). This may seem to be a veiled authorial comment about V.'s attempt with regard to Sebastian himself and that V. 's biography is thus "fictitious even though it contains some objective facts" (*RLSK* 41). Echoing Sebastian's way of composing a fictitious biography, V. is possible to get some inspiration from this and tries to write a fictitious biography about Sebastian with Sebastian's novels and autobiography as his essential material. Combining these details and analyzing them, we see the fictional construction on the part of V. is obvious. Though we cannot prove or disprove if V. and Sebastian are actually related, this uncertain relationship refuses to make anything settled and continues to cast doubts on the ontological identity of both V. and Sebastian.

Being fictitious on Sebastian's real life and V. 's half-brother role, *The Real Life of Sebastian Knight* is Nabokov's another book of the conscious construction of the working of the soul of the dead man under intellectual/literary camouflage. In it, the narrator/writer V. of the biography consciously constructs a ghostly relationship between himself and the dead man's soul and seems to be mysteriously guided by the soul of the dead Sebastian and by his "private labyrinth" (*RLSK* 187). For Nabokov, patterning in human life reflects fate and implies the otherworld. As Cincinnatus and his mother share at least something ingenious and unique that is beyond the mundane people's cognition, V. and his half-brother also are connected through some ghostly pattern. Of his interview with Sebastian's Cambridge friend, V. says "Sebastian's spirit seemed to hover about us" (*RLSK* 50) and he announces that Sebastian is "peering unseen" over his shoulder as he writes (*RLSK* 56). When V. went to Sebastian's flat and flipped through the dozen dresses hanging in the wardrobe, he "had an odd impression of Sebastian's body being stiffly multiplied in a succession of square-shouldered forms" (*RLSK* 36). Staying in Sebastian's flat, V. says that "for a moment I seemed to see a transparent Sebastian at his desk; or rather I thought of that passage about the wrong Roquebrune: perhaps he preferred doing his writing in bed" (*RLSK* 39)? Being influenced by Sebastian's own experience, V. is consciously following the workings of Sebastian's thoughts in similar situations so as to reproduce a sensibility that is connected with Sebastian's in an occult way.

The most revealing episode of the occult relationship between V. and

Sebastian's soul is described in V. 's arrival at the hospital in St. Damier. V
does not know that Sebastian has died some hours earlier, and makes the mistake of sitting for a few minutes by another man's sickbed. During this time he
manages to obtain the most intimate understanding of his half-brother and he
feels that his life is changed. Though he later realizes his error of mistaking another man for his already dead brother, he still insists that there is a spiritual
connection between them: "Thus—I am Sebastian Knight" (*RLSK* 205). This
revelation on the part of V. in the last chapter is coincident with Sebastian's
spiritual discovery in the first chapter—his communion with his dead mother's
soul though he was meditating at the wrong hotel that his mother stayed before
death. The similarities involved in these two scenes in the beginning and ending
by both Sebastian the biographee and V. the biographer connect the two naturally and fatefully in an occult way. This occult echoing seems to V. a conscious
realization of Sebastian's spiritual discovery and he seems to replace Sebastian
in both his verbal art and metaphysical ideas near the end of the book. For Sebastian, there seems to be a predetermined pattern for him to follow both in his
life and his art. His life seems to be entangled with his dead mother in an omi-
nous way and his art is concerned with the occult unknown related with love,
fateful artifice and death. As Sebastian's friend Sheldon the poet says about *The
Doubtful Asphodel* that this last book "was already casting its shadows on all
things surrounding him [Sebastian] and that his novels and stories were but
bright masks, sly tempters under the pretense of artistic adventure leading him
unerringly towards a certain imminent goal" (*RLSK* 104). Through this, we
see that Sebastian's life and art are coordinate with each other and both of them
follow a fateful course that is unconsciously at first and then consciously realized by Sebastian himself.

　　For V. , there also seems to be a predetermined pattern that he can not escape from. The facts that he had dug out about Sebastian's life appear to fit into a
preexisting pattern. He says that his quest "has developed its own magic and logic" (*RLSK* 137). An example is his discovery that there is a law of some strange
harmony in the placing of Sebastian's first love affairs with his last dark love. The
reason is that he was led by a chance remark of Helene Gristein to a meeting

with "Rosanov's sister" —Natasha Rosanov—the adolescent love while Helene Gristein was formerly supposed to be one of the four possible dark lady candidates that V. is determined to check and interview one by one. The juxtaposition of the first loves and the last dark love are seen by V. as the "harmony" that he discovers and believes that they are set down in his text out of some other power's making. There is a gradual acknowledgement of the pattern preexisted there in the text. The possible reason that it is not openly declared is that the reader is not paying attention to these signs scattered by V. in the texts. Only when we reread can we establish the connections among them. In the earlier part, V.'s remarks of explanation of his doing this and not doing are more or less rational though they are sometimes tinged with his subjective bias in constructing the book the way he intends. But then when he comes to the matters that are beyond his rational explanation such as Sebastian's intimate feelings and memories about his dead mother, V. either quotes the words of Sebastian or constructs his own version of illustration based on the reason that they are brothers, sharing the same rhythm. Therefore, like Sebastian in another diegetic level, V. is following some pattern in writing the biography. Like what V. says in the latter half of the novel: "That quest [the writing of this biography], using the pattern of reality for the weaving of its own fancies, I am forced to recognize that I was being led right, and that in striving to render Sebastian's life I must now follow the same rhythmical interlacements" (*RLSK* 137). The fragments and episodes are all realities around which the fancy things are woven. Therefore, the justification of V. as a narrator at the early parts of the book as the traditional narrators have always done are now consciously realized by V. as the fateful pattern concerning the selection and arrangement of the materials of Sebastian's life.

Being a narrator and a writer, V. can share Sebastian through the interlacements and inner rhythm that we have discussed in the above. As a reader of Sebastian's books, V. is also the kind of reader that Nabokov favors and claims as the good reader in his *Lectures in Literature*. First, V. unlike the traditional readers, does not believe in the realities represented in the literary texts and does not take them literally and unimaginatively. He regards the "real" that Sebastian has depicted as authentic or high art. He ridicules Mr. Goodman as a bad reader in his literal and unimaginative reading and interpretation of Sebastian's texts. "Keeping a note-book where he jotted down certain remarks of his employer—and apparently some of these related to his employer's past," (*RLSK* 63) Mr. Goodman as described by V. literally reads Sebastian's jokes, word-pictures and anecdotes. As in Nabokov's view, "authentic or high art is never false, in the sense of being gratuitously unrelated to the author's experiences or the world in which he lives, even if it makes no attempt to faithfully mirror 'reality' (which is both meaningless and impossible in Nabokov's conception)" (Alexandrov, *Nabokov's Otherworld* 145). For Nabokov, it is imagination that relies on memory and inspiration that yields not mere fantasy but truth (or fantasy that is plausible in the terms of the Pushkin lecture). With this unique understanding of the "real", V. makes fun of Mr. Goodman and ridicules his unimaginative interpretations of Sebastian's playful jokes, ironies and appropriations in a verisimilitude context in his *The Tragedy of Sebastian Knight.*

Second, he reads Sebastian's texts with a consciousness toward Sebastian's romantic irony. Rather than falling into the traps that are set up by the fanciful and sentimental descriptions at the first reading for the careless readers, V. seems to share the sensibilities of Sebastian and leads the reader most of the time in a right track. In the romantic scenes and outpouring emotions in Sebastian's texts, there is always a tinge of ugliness, vulgarity and unromanticism waiting in there, deflating the overwhelming sensations. For the careless readers, these are always neglected. Vice verse, in those episodes where the "serious feelings" of the human being concerning the dead mother in Mr. Goodman's eyes, Sebastian speaks in a very reserved way, seemingly uninvolved, but actually poignant. These, likewise, can only be figured out by the readers whose excessive romantic feelings have been calmed down while his deepened sense of humanism pervades everywhere in a more profound sense. Third, V. is also an imaginative reader who knows that the aesthetic bliss is achieved through the revelation of both the writer and the reader. The reader, or rather the rereader, for Nabokov, is the party through which his artistic ideas and unique understanding of the world and art are realized. Thus, to cultivate the readers' aesthetic taste for literature and art is always his major concern. The reading method and the composing method of V. are seen as a very good means to demonstrate his ideas and thoughts in art. Being a narrator, a writer and a reader, V., through his fictional and imaginative construction of Sebastian's life and art, produces the book itself which is the real life of Sebastian Knight. The emphasis of the fictionality of the book itself is the foregrounding of the idea that high art is never false and the imagination and artistic creativity are the truth where a pattern or fateful plan is hidden behind.

IV   A Space of Mimicry Constructed for Nabokov's Speaking Self

For Nabokov, true art does not serve any worldly purpose. True art delights the mind and this happens in nature too. Both art and nature are non-utilitarian in that they both contain the non-utilitarian character—mimicry. Mimicry usually is said to serve the purpose of protecting an animal from predators, but according to Nabokov it may be so staggeringly subtle and refined that it exceeds the predator's powers of discrimination. Thus, there is an aesthetic surplus in mimicry that the mimic has no use for and that thus there is more to mimicry than can be explained by its uses. (Grayson 49) For Nabokov, mimicry in nature is a source of constant wonderment. For Nabokov, the fascination with observable detail as well as with disguise and deception is also one of the intangible links between art and nature. Art is for Nabokov deception, disguises and artifice that are laid out for camouflaging some patterns. As we observe nature, the disguises and deceptions in Nabokov's art are set in such a subtle way that they surpass the mere function of story-telling, characterization and plot development, transcending the artistic conventions so as to deliver his pattern—a well mapped-out otherworld power hidden in his texts. The details of certain images, the settings, the atmosphere and numbers are repeated, recombined and remodelled, correlating to form a meaningful pattern, a higher consciousness or the soul of the dead man in the protagonist's quest. Going beyond the mere show of verbal style, Nabokov is laying out his otherworld pattern and theme through a combination of details and signs that produce both a sensually vivid world of art and a meta-physical pattern underneath it.

In *The Real Life of Sebastian Knight*, Nabokov uses the metafictional world of mimicry and deception to express his metaphysical pattern. To express his ideas and concerns with the otherworld power in our life, Nabokov in this book depicts a story-in-story framework to quest through his character for the remotest truth of the otherworld. Setting up a half-brother relationship between V. and Sebastian, Nabokov prepares from the very beginning for the inter-reflections between the two, one alive, living in the mundane world and the other dead, leaving his artistic works behind. Having blood connection, V. seems to have access to Sebastian's inner rhythm. With the relationship between this side and the other side of the boundary between life and death established, Nabokov moves to let V. take a journey to collect those details related with Sebastian in physical and spiritual, literary and metaphysical ways. Travelling in the shadows and being led through intuition by the soul of Sebastian, V. moves to construct the world of an artist—Sebastian who is following his own unknowable intuitions and fateful life course in both life and literary works. Projecting his innermost cognitions toward literature and metaphysical questions of love, death and the ideal world onto V. , the dead Sebastian is speaking through the living V. in the most camouflaged way. When V. is carrying out his mission in collecting Sebastian's life facts, he feels that Sebastian is peering at him, unseen over his shoulder. When V. is telling the stories about Sebastian, he warns the reader of the three-fold fictionalities in them. Even though V. finds it hard to understand Sebastian's sudden drop-off of the relationship with Clare and sought hopeless and disastrous love from a Russian lady—Nina, he chooses the right and insightful passage from Sebastian's books and hints at Sebastian's fateful life that somewhat echoes his early descriptions of Sebastian's mother's capricious character. Stepping into Sebastian's position, V. reflects Sebastian's air and mood, but with his own constructions.

Nabokov is known, as it is the case in Sebastian, for his appropriations of his own life facts, his past memories and his understanding of literary tradition in his art. To apply these to the characters and the events in their lives, Nabokov chooses to create a fictional world in which a scholar is experiencing the very process of writing a biography of a prestigious late writer. However, the way that Nabokov transfers his major concerns as we see in his life and understanding of art is very deceptive and mimetic in that he takes pains to design two fictional worlds, one embedded in the other with careful details to camouflage his true intensions. Creating two diegetic levels of narrative, Nabokov makes the two characters in two different ontological worlds while Nabokov is detached from these two, further removed from the essence of the flashy Sebastian. Thus, the novel is more fictional than the traditional novels in that it lays bare the working of the composing of the book on the part of V. who is all along conscious of himself as a writer of fiction. In addition, the fictional world composed by V. is also presenting another fictional world in which Sebastian and his fellow characters are living. In Sebastian's world, things tend to be more dreamy and unreal. Those things related with Sebastian's love and death appear even more evasive and occult though V. tries hard to wring the possible truth from Sebastian's literary works. The relationship between Sebastian's life and his fictional works is now forced to the fore and we the readers also have to consider its innate reflection of each other. For an ingenious writer as Sebastian, he will never allow his life facts to be straight-forwardly presented in his works. But at the same time, as we are told, Sebastian is a writer that has the ability to transform the ideas and thoughts he is toying with in his real life into his fictional characters, even those grotesque ones. The imagination and artistic creativity involved in this recombination of the facts and fictionality are the very uniqueness of Sebastian's art, differing from those fellow writers and critics who write and review the novels for their political ideas, social positions and commonsense functions of morality. Removed from V. and further from V. 's biographee, Nabokov is not to be easily and directly detected in terms of his intrusions and artifice in the text, thus leaving his "real" intentions even more fictional and more ambiguous as he has intended from the very start.

Being pushed to the fore, the problem of the relationship of fictionality and the facts of life is three times reflected: it is reflected in Sebastian's case; it is also reflected in V. 's case; and it is further reflected in Nabokov's dealing with the same problem. Here Nabokov's emphasis is not difficult to detect when we cast off layer by layer his deceptive artifice. By creating these three layers of artistic worlds (the writer's, the narrator's and the character's worlds), he is discussing his aesthetic concerns with the problem of the "real" and the reality, the artistic construction and verisimilitude representation. To justify his belief that only the subjective and artistic imagination of the details and the memories of remote past are the valid elements in high and authentic art, Nabokov creates a space in which three literary worlds inter-reflect each other, one leading the other to follow the traces of the more fictional one to prove how impossible it is to pin down the real. In addition, the past, though gloomy and depressed, is regained in a positive way through the recalling of the mind with the sensitivity of the artistic artifice. Further, the dead is made alive in guiding the living to live the pattern that offers a new way of looking at the mundane world and thus achieving the happiness that one can only find in the otherworld. In this literary space well set by Nabokov, time is transformed into space in that the linear line of time is replaced by a spiral that forms a forever upward twirling space around that former time line that is non-existent now, repeating the past while combining the present new so as to form a new base from which another arc is started. This spiral being formed, the boundary of the past and the present is broken and the confinement of time is thus being transcended through this cosmic synchronization.

As Alexandrov rightly reviewed, Nabokov in his *Speak, Memory* hints at the idea that his practice of cosmic synchronization provides him intermittent escape from the prison of time and a possible life after death (*The Garland Companion* 48). To drive this idea home, Nabokov in *The Real Life of Sebastian Knight* makes V. describe Sebastian as if time does not exist for Sebastian. To criticize against Mr. Goodman's fallacious assertion in his biography *The Tragedy of Sebastian Knight* that Sebastian was influenced by the historical moment in which he lives, V says that "time for Sebastian was never 1914 or 1920 or1936—it was always year 1" (*RLSK* 65). Freeing himself from the time confinement, Sebastian can use his art of multi-level thinking to strive for the otherworld life. In the attitude toward the great human catastrophes, Sebastian cannot understand why people should be less troubled by catastrophes in the distant past than in the present. Therefore, V. concludes that "time and space were to [Sebastian] measure of the same eternity, so that the very idea of his reacting in any special 'modern' way to what Mr. Goodman calls 'the atmosphere of postwar Europe' is utterly preposterous" (*RLSK* 66). In the fiction *The Doubtful Asphodel*, Sebastian describes time and space as "childish terms" that are "riddles invented by man *as* riddles" (*RLSK* 178). And his reference to the entire span of the man's existence as "the kindergarten of life" further implies that after death he will enter not only into a "full-grown" state of being but one in which the childish earthly conception of time will no longer be relevant. (Alexandrov, *Nabokov's Otherworld* 142) Inspired by Sebastian's artistic practice of timelessness, V. realizes that he has traveled far enough to follow the pattern and logic of Sebastian, shrugging off the burden of time confinement in quest of a new possible way of looking at this world.

Introducing this timeless space to the character—Sebastian and arming his half-brother V. with the epiphany and inspiration from Sebastian, Nabokov reasserts his idea of the "real" as something that can transcend the mundane and childish understandings of time so as to bring alive the pattern of the otherworld in the remotest character. In this artistic space, Nabokov puts his fatidic "watermark" of the otherworld sensibility onto the dead Sebastian with his spirit now emerge and now hide alternatively to pervade the whole text rendered by the living V.. The details that Nabokov cherishes in this artistic world resemble the mimicry in nature in that they are created not simply for utilitarian purpose of rendering a storyline and characters. They go beyond these practical functions to combine and unite so as to meet the preexisting pattern. Scattering in the text various signs, trivialities and those brief appearances of some minor characters, Nabokov lays out deliberately different links among those seemingly unrelated details for the reader to reread so as to discover their inner connections and the fateful powers working underneath.

Expressed through words, Nabokov's idea of this preexist pattern seems to have something to do with what could be called Platonic conception of art. In Sebastian's struggle with writing, Nabokov implants his own concern about the verbal expression of the thought of the otherworld in the description of V. about Sebastian: "the maddening feeling that the right words, the only words are awaiting for you on the opposite bank in the misty distance," which is balanced by "the shudderings of the still unclothed thought clamouring for them on this side of the abyss" (*RLSK* 84). This description of the thoughts to meet the "right words" on the opposite bank implies that the very construction of the work—the words united with thoughts preexist their being set down by the writer. V. 's remarks of Sebastian's maddening feeling are also echoed by Sebastian's own description in *The Doubtful Asphodel*. In it, Sebastian described the impossibility of man's understanding as to what lies beyond death as Fyordor in *The Gift* quotes from Delanlande that life is like a house and death as the landscape beyond (Alexandrov, *Nabokov's Otherworld* 142). Sebastian's maddening feeling to quest for the meaning after death is expressed only by what we can know: "only one half of the notion of death can be said really to exist: *this* side of the question—the wrench, the parting, the quay of life gently moving away aflutter with handkerchiefs" (*RLSK* 177). The camouflage of words is finally aiming at something inexpressible, something working in an invisible way, everywhere and nowhere.

The preexisting pattern that Nabokov is concerned is also exemplified in V. 's approach toward Sebastian's death and his quest for Sebastian's lethal last love. When we follow V. 's quest, we feel that Sebastian's novels somehow anticipate V. 's search or that V. 's search somehow reenacts Sebastian's novels. With our reading, we feel more and more hopeful in deriving the reason of this crescendo of echoes as the book itself approaches the end with the promise of an all-deciding disclosure from the dying Sebatian——and that in turn mimics the pattern of Sebastian's last novel (Boyd, *The Russian Years* 498). Listening to the sleeping patient breathing, V. experiences a profound spiritual communion. But it all turns out to be an embarrassing mistake. After he spelled out "knight" in agitation and explained "It's an English name," (*RLSK* 207) the French sanatorium staff had directed him to the unlit bedside of someone called Kegan. The nurse exclaims "Oh-la-la" when she realizes the error and embarrassingly says "The Russian gentleman dies yesterday" (*RLSK* 208). Here the novel closes, with V. declaring that "those few minutes I spent listening to what I thought was his breathing" (*RLSK* 208) have changed his life completely, for he has learned "that the soul is but a manner of being—not a constant state—that any soul may be yours, if you find and follow its undulations ··· Thus—I am Sebastian Knight···or Sebastian Kinght is I, or perhaps we both are someone whom neither of us knows" (*RLSK* 211). It is possible that V. is so immersed in his life-long quest for the real life of Sebastian that he has a tinge of madness in himself. But Sebastian's last book was also a fictitious biography. The parodic biography of *The Real Life of Sebastian Knight* seems to match the tone and the innovative strategies of Sebastian's own work. In addition, both V. and Sebastian write in English, but at the last moment Sebastian proves to be inescapably the Russian that V. has been all along. It is only the letter *v* that distinguishes the Russian "Sebvastian" from English "Sebastian". (Boyd, *The Russian Years* 498)

Reflecting and reenacting each other in their works, V. and Sebastian are one and the same with V.'s stepping into Sebastian's soul and with the only difference of the letter *v*. This inner-echoing between the book of V. and the last book of Sebastian emerges now out of the clustering of all these details and the reader can, through drawing textual connections, figure out that the book—*The Real Life of Sebastian Knight* is guided by the last book of Sebastian, reworking Sebastian's life of art and love in another sphere. This interpretation can be further reinforced by the brief appearance of a character called Silbermann. When V. appears to find it impossible to search out Sebastian's lover and decides that he may have to paint a deliberately incomplete portrait of Sebastian, he meets a person named Silbermann who offers help to him. Silbermann within a week produces him a name list of those who stayed in the hotel where Sebastian was supposed to stay in 1929. This name list not only helps V. find Sebastian's first Russian love—Natasha Rosanov about whom V. formerly has not any knowledge and whose love with Sebastian in a large way explains Sebastian's obsession with his last dark love—the Russian lady Nina Rechnoy. It also produces the clue of Sebastian's last dark lover—Nina. But when we look closely at Silbermann, he is not a real person in V.'s narrative world. Rather, he is a fictional character from one of Sebastian's books. Being a helper, Sibermann, coming from Sebastian's book, guides V. in his search and this episode, in a way, seems to prove that Sebastian is consciously living in V. 's soul and guides him through his work and spirit to take the right move.

In addition, Sebastian's capriciousness in his love affairs can be explained when we put it in the context of V. 's approaching Sebastian's death. Though having a very happy relationship with Clare Bishop who seems to be doomed in her own right in London, Sebastian cuts the relationship off when he discovers that he has inherited his mother's fatal angina. Since then, he becomes restless and leaves her to pursue another woman who has a disastrous effect on him. His morbid obsession toward the dark lady of Russia is anticipated by his failure in his first love affair with Natasha back in Russia. This first love and the dark love are connected by some power or pattern in V. 's biography and it dawns upon V. that it is the book itself that develops its own logic and reason to lead him to connect the two women together by putting them one immediately after another. On the other hand, Sebastian's mysterious abandoning of Clare Bishop for that disastrous woman needs to be examined by drawing Nabokov himself into the context. Taking up about one third of the book, V. 's search for Sebastian's last lover can not be neglected. After many obstacles and delays, V. finally began to pin down Sebastian's mysterious lover—Nina who tells her own story by faking telling some other person's story just as V. is none other than Sebastian telling about himself. Or this "someone whom neither of us knows" may be the author talking about himself in a way that disguises his personal disclosure (Boyd, *The Russian Years* 500). What Nabokov himself is involved personally may be his change of language and his burying of his past with Irina Guadanini (Boyd, *The Russian Years* 501).

When V. 's dissolving into Sebastian and Sebastian's dissolving into Nabokov can be seen more clearly at this stage of discussion, we can interpret Sebastian's first idyll with Natasha on the quiet water of a Russian river recalling of Nabokov's own first love for Valentina Shulgin to whom he addressed all of his early Russian verse back in 1915. According to Nabokov's biographer—Boyd, Nabokov declares obliquely that while his mind tells him he ought now to remain an English writer; his heart urges him back, against all prudence, to the charms of his Russian muse. In *The Real Life of Sebastian Knight*, V. finds in the things left by the dead Sebastian a letter written in Russian and caught a line before the letter is swallowed by the fire set to burn them: "thy manners always to find" (*RLSK* 38). V. admits that "it is not the sense that struck me, but the mere fact of its being in my language" (*RLSK* 38). This detail may pass the reader's attention. But when this is considered along with V. 's exclamation of Sebastian's incomparably excellent and rich Russian and the dying Sebastian's last letter to V. written in Russian, we cannot help relating this with Nabokov's obsession to his mother tongue. And we cannot forget his staying in Cambridge for four years composing Russian verses and taking Russian literature as his major. His fear of throwing away his asset in his literary works accompanied him to his stay in Berlin and France after Cambridge years. His unceasing efforts in translating and commenting Pushkin's work *Eugene Onegin* were also his extended concern with Russian language. By the time he finished his *The Real Life of Sebastian Knight* in January, 1939, he was on the verge of immigrating into America. Being his first English novel, *The Real Life of Sebastian Knight* does contain some autobiographical sketches of a Russian's early association with England which he had already written about that time. Boyd suggests that these sketches of London combined with Nabokov's recent impressions of literary London provide the germ of this English novel (Boyd, *The Russian Years* 496).

In Nabokov's novel, this Russian tinge is reflected in both Mme Lercerf (Nina in disguise) who feigns not to be Russian and Sebastian who also pretends not to be Russian on Cambridge Campus and after his London years. There are descriptions of Mme Lercerf who mixes her English words with French and Sebastian's foreign appearance and his Russian "lapsing into English as soon as the conversation drew out to anything longer than a couple of sentences" (*RLSK* 31). But Sebastian is finally what he is: he is classed as the "Russian gentleman" in the sanitarium where he dies. This complex of Russian language is materialized in this novel in that V. , against his own will, in order to recount the life of an English writer who can not cut his Russian ties, has to use English language to write the book. This book, *The Real Life of Sebastian Knight* as

Nabokov's first English book, can also be understood as a book transforming his agony and pain suffered in reality into art. In addition, Nabokov's extra-marital love affair with Irina is also transformed into the book. As Boyd remarks, Nabokov in his own life hoped that his letter to her would be destroyed after his request to Irina Guadanini as Sebastian has required V. having his love letters to Nina destroyed (ibid. 501). Burying his past with Irina and leaving his great agony of abandoning Russian language in his artistic space, Nabokov creates *The Real Life of Sebastian Knight* in such a self-reflexive and self-contained way so as to pin it down there in a space of mimicry, the fateful pattern working there, camouflaged by the artistic deception.

Chapter III   The Speaking "I" Reinscribed In-between Personal Life and Impersonal Art in *Speak, Memory*

The book *Speak, Memory: an Autobiography Revisited* is based on a series of sketches that Nabokov wrote from 1936 to 1951. As it is said by Nabokov himself in the preface of this autobiography, the book is "a systematically correlated assemblage of personal recollections ranging geographically from St. Petersburg to St. Nazaire, and covering thirty-seven years, from August 1903 to May 1940, with only a few sallies into later space-time" (*SM* 9). To explore further about the features of this autobiography, we need to examine the evolution of the book's aim and purpose on the part of Nabokov. In 1946, Nabokov went back to the project started with "Mademoiselle O" a decade earlier. He published fourteen more autobiographical sketches, mostly in *The New Yorker*, which concentrated on his boyhood and youth in Russia and then moved more quickly through his European years. After making some revisions, Nabokov put the sketches together to make a fifteen-chapter autobiography entitled *Conclusive Evidence* in the year 1951. Later it was renamed *Speak, Memory*. In *Selected Letters*, Nabokov offers us his plans for *Speak, Memory* in his 1946 prospectus. In this prospectus, with "Mademoiselle O" as his model for both the cross-cultural subject matter and the autobiographical method, Nabokov makes it clear that he plans a book that would "involve the picturing of many different lands and peoples and modes of living" (*SL* 69). In John Foster's review, Nabokov's later prospectus of 1948 made a more specialized notion of culture in his attempt of the book, (Foster 179) saying that the book should be

"an inquiry into the elements that have gone to form my personality as a writer"
(*SL* 88). With the emphasis on multiculturalism, Nabokov tends to draw his art
and memory in his autobiography in an international cultural context so as to begin a new kind of autobiography.

In his autobiography as he declared in his early 1946 prospectus, Nabokov
is not trying to show the absolute individuality of the individual, the determined
quest for the mnemonic image to originality. (Foster 179) Rather, the peculi-
arity of his book will lie in its tricky use of fictional elements so that it will not
be a pure autobiography but "rather a new hybrid between that and a novel"
(*SL* 69). But this is later changed in his letter to Edmund Wilson written in
1947 in terms of the art-memory problematic. With his great concern toward scientific precision in searching out his present self, he declares that his autobiography will be "a scientific attempt to unravel and trace back all the tangled
threads of one's personality" (*NWL* 188). But here he seems to say in this exag-
gerated way to disagree with Wilson's comment of his "Mademoiselle O" as
"beautifully written" (*NWL* 188). But anyway, the 1948 prospectus shows a
middle way of writing his past in artistic form as "the blending of perfect personal truth with strict artistic selection" (*SL* 88). As to the possible failures in ac-
curacy about his past, it is due to "the frailty of memory, not to the trickery of
art" as indicated in Nabokov's "Author's Note" to *Conclusive Evidence.* (*CE*
vii) Based on these claims, we can see that while the accurateness of the recollection is emphasized, the participation of artistic construction is seen as playing
an important role in shaping the past of the author.

Nabokov's concern of the role of artistic construction in his autobiography is
underscored whenever he discusses revising his essays and sketches to combine
them into an artistically united autobiography. As John Foster pointed out, there
are two problems that have to be tackled in transforming the sketches into the
book-length autobiography: that of continuity from chapter to chapter, and that
of providing an adequate conclusion. (Foster 179) If these essays are simply
piled with each other, the lack of continuity will result in "a sequence of short
essay-like bits" (*SL* 69) and it is what for Nabokov should be avoided. In his
1948 prospectus, Nabokov proposes to make some alterations so as to make

"the flow of the book ··· more ample and sustained" (*SL* 88). But except for some interconnections of characters and episodes among the chapters, few revisions actually take place. It might be due to the reason that Nabokov finally intends to follow the rhythm of his memories and justify the importance of the past, their own vitality and flow by preserving the traces of the discontinuity of them. This flow of the memory on its own is shown in the positions of the episodes and fragments in the text. They move back and forth through time and recur in various forms and contexts in local parts where necessary. Despite these temporal dislocations, these episodes of the memories basically follow the linear procession and the overall arrangements of the chapters proceed basically from the dawning of his consciousness to his marriage, fatherhood and his ready departure of the European continent for America, following the linear structure in a large way.

As to the providing of an adequate conclusion, Nabokov does not actually include it in the final version of the book. As he said in his 1946 prospectus, closure would be done by an abrupt change of perspective, so that the serialized fragments "suddenly gathering momentum will form into something very weird and dynamic" (*SL* 69). And in a November 1949 letter to his editor Katherine White, he mentions a planned chapter 16 to emphasize the artistic structure of this notion. In the planned chapter 16, Nabokov in the letter talks about shifting from the first-persona autobiographical narrator into a third person and discusses the point of view from a fictitious reviewer. Though Nabokov actually wrote it, he did not add it into the final version of the book since his notion of identifying and analyzing "the various themes running through the book—all the intricate threads I have been at pains to follow through each piece" (*SL* 95) is repeated in each chapter. In this way, after giving full exemplification of his past, the whole momentum suddenly changes when it comes near to the end of most chapters. There Nabokov voices his important new insights about his art of memory and writes in a poetic way his artistic imagination and insightful epiphany accumulated through the recalling of the past. In addition, there is a play of perspectives as striking as the shift from first-person to third person in the context where Nabokov shifts abruptly from the narrated to the authorial self in exercising his autobiographer's privilege. In this way, the rhythm of the past is followed while the artifice connects the fragments by epiphanic moments, accumulative effects and conscious construction and comments of the author. Therefore, with the fragmented episodes of the past being respected and followed, Nabokov creates a more diffused pattern which combines the details of the past and the illuminations of the present. To present the whole book through a natural undulation of factual details of the past and the resulted inspiring heaving of the emotions, Nabokov gives his memories the utmost systematic play in his autobiography through conscious authorial construction. In his "dialogue" between his art and his life in *Speak*, *Memory*, Nabokov chooses to parallel his unique art with his unique life of exile, at the same time, the two interlace with each other and complement each other to reach the artistic summit not without Nabokov's emphasis on the haunted power of his past and his true life episodes.

When Nabokov is asked what he means that he loses the sense of a memory once having written it down, Nabokov answers that he divides his memories into two kinds: intellectual memory and emotional memory. The intellectual memory loses its sense once it is being written down, but not for the emotional one. The emotional memory refers to something such as the freshness of the flowers being arranged by the under-gardener as he is running down the stairs with the butterfly net on a summer day half a century ago. This kind of emotional memory is permanent and immortal. (*SO* 12) No matter how many times he entrusts these memories to his characters, they are always there as permanent possessions. Dividing memories into these two kinds, Nabokov consciously distinguishes the temporary memories and those permanent ones, the latter influencing his life and art in a profound way. Those memories play important roles in evoking Nabokov's understanding of the world, its time, space, otherworld, love, his exiled life and humanities. In Nabokov's eyes, the relationship between the author and the world transferred from the art is the first-class art rather than the relationship of the characters in the work as clearly indicated by Nabokov in his *Speak*, *Memory*. Giving them full space in the book, Nabokov shapes his consciousness and the related understandings of the outside world through the summing up of his life in an artistic framework, best showing forth the insinuations and the relationship of his self and his art, his self-identity and the world at large. Emphasizing the emotional side of the memories that carry out his life-long interests and devotions, Nabokov combines the emotion that is attached to the mnemonic fragments of the past with his artistic elevations achieved through his literary artifice, thus melting one into the other to write an autobiography that coalesces factual and fictional, personal and impersonal, past and present.

In the arrangement of the themes of this book, Nabokov mainly writes four different themes that cover his life up to age 40. The book starts with the family circle that Nabokov recalls around his boyhood and adolescence. The first three chapters and parts of chapter 9 and 10 are devoted to the details of his parents, uncle, his cousin Yuri. In these, the theme of Nabokov's early memories are presented in a large context of culture while contemplating issues related to literature, language, family love, memories, consciousness and his awareness of his artistic position. Then it moves to the multicultural educations that Nabokov receives from his governesses, tutors and later the secondary and university education. In chapter 4, 5, 8 and 13 as well as part of chapter 9 are dealing with them and talk about the French, English, and Russian cultural influences that Nabokov has had. These educations enlighten Nabokov and lead him into his major life concerns and interests. After an insertion of education of painting, the book focuses on literature and science. This third theme is discussed in chapter 6, 11 and 14 and it is also anticipated in chapter 2, 4, and 5. The fourth theme is about Nabokov's emotional romance, beginning with his early loves in chapter 7, part of 10, and 12 and then moving to marriage and fatherhood in last chapter—chapter 15.

These thematic topics scattered in the book contain Nabokov's four major images that have immense relationship with his art—Nabokov's earliest memories, French governess, the butterflies and Nabokov's father. Running all through the book and connecting these images in the book are Nabokov's love toward his wife, addressing her as "you" most prominently in the last chapter while at the footstep of moving with his wife and son toward their new life in America. This present life status of Nabokov with his wife and son, serving as the most external narrative framework and connecting Nabokov's past, present and future, encloses within itself another theme, the theme of Nabokov's love toward his father that is also seen emerging from time and time, all through the whole book. The theme of his father is also connected with Nabokov's theme of butterfly, his belief in otherworld, his love of literature and language as well as his liberal outlook and moral standing point. Starting to take a great delight in butterfly from his father, Nabokov transfers his love of entomology and his precision and exactness into his verbal art. His artistically constructed ideal space in his works is thus inevitably connected with his love toward his late father and then further connected with his positive construction of his otherworld sensibility that returns to affirm his living life. And the beauty of butterfly and moth and their nirvana in a more unique sense intensifies this belief in the otherworld.

In this, Nabokov's love toward his mother is also closely connected with Nabokov's belief of otherworld, his affirmation of love and his will to happiness while holding belief in the fateful power of life since his mother holds that there is an afterlife after death and the construction of the good and positive things in the past can bring one an eternal happiness in whatever harsh and desperate living situation. Inherited from his mother is also the nostalgic sensibility—the love of the past, the unique way of combining color and words— "colored hearing" and the power of love. The color sensation combines the pictorial with the verbal, drawing connection between Nabokov's painting classes in his life and his love of words in his art. The power of love that is shared by both his father and mother is fully felt by Nabokov. Nabokov says that all poetry is positional; trying to "express one's position in regard to the universe embraced by consciousness is an immemorial urge" (SM 218). Through feeling everything that happens at one point of time, Nabokov uses the term "cosmic synchronization" to define his position through his conscious love toward his family in this autobiography. Joining love and art, Nabokov makes his art conscious and eternal, modern and romantic. With these inspiring images as the cores of the autobiography and their interconnections with each other, Speak, Memory records the details of Nabokov's facts of life around these glowing and glimmering coals in the darkness, arranging details that aim to disclose the epiphanies that Nabokov accumulates through the course of recalling the past and the associations of the pictorial and the verbal, the personal life and the impersonal art.

For Nabokov's earliest memories around his boyhood and adolescence, *Speak*, *Memory* shows Nabokov's unique way of looking at the world. His colored hearing, his love of memories in his remote past and his belief of the afterlife are all touched upon to be seen as having close relationship with his mother. These ensure him a no-ordinary life and an art that magnifies the triviality and minimizes the big significances so that all things become equally important. Closely connected with his art, Nabokov's life of education offered by his tutors is best exemplified in an independent short story entitled "Mademoiselle O" and later is added into the book, talking about a Swiss lady whose French language and culture have great impact upon the young Nabokov. Delivered from this part is Nabokov's eternalized image of his Swiss governess whom he revisited years later after she returns to her country. Recreating his memory with the help of his artistic imagination and self-conscious construction, Nabokov infuses his art and memory, the impersonal and personal to construct a unified image of his past, fixed eternally through his conscious artistic strategy. Not being a separate, "cognitive" activity in his life, entomology is associated with Nabokov's art of memory and its origins in synesthesia. His quest for the exact and precise details in his art is an extension of his love of the butterflies. The insights connected with and derived from the butterflies are reinforced by his conscious construction of the pattern of art. From a boyhood, his hobby of butterflies and moths has become a scientific vocation by the time Nabokov wrote his autobiography. The pursuit of butterflies and moths is related with Nabokov's art in the retrieval of mnemonic images while their colorful wings can be viewed as an emblem of colored hearing. (Foster 183)

Being paralleled with Nabokov's art, butterfly pursuit involves in itself the regaining of the details of the past as if seeing through a microscope and Nabokov's concern of finding a new species and then naming it as related with his concern of the proper names and definitions of words in his art. Nabokov's obsession with discovering a new species corresponds to that urge for literary modernity which impels him to revise or even attack the author being imitated. (Foster 184) This quest for butterfly is further likened to Nabokov's interest toward the mimicry in nature and his extended viewpoint of the mimicry in art where deception is the non-utilitarian art that is designed by the artist simply to satisfy and delight. This deception of art in Nabokov is again related to his love of chess and his painstaking efforts paid toward the inventing of the compositions and solutions of the chess problems. The thetic, the anti-thetic and the synthetic are the three steps that Nabokov designs not only to tackle with the art of chess but also to summarize his life process. In designing the deception in the solution of the chess problems, Nabokov tends to use deception in chess problem to cheat the other party into his trap and thus reach his real aim and gain his solution. This is not unlike his deception in his art where he sets traps to cover his real intentions since he believes that art is deception. The use of these three terms is again related with Nabokov's depiction of his life in exile, thus interconnecting life and art in this spiral form. Along with all these images, Nabokov, through referring recurrently to his father all along the text, self-consciously pins down the immemorial image and portraits of his father in separate contexts. These different occurrences of his father evoke both the most significant moment of his father being tossed into the air and the funeral, having spanned more than a decade in his father's life. In this sense, the description of his father, as the pivot of the recollection, transcends time by freezing a single instant/moment and remains eternal along with the images that carry Nabokov's lifelong urge and desires.

Transforming these images of his life concerns into something free from time confinement, Nabokov wisely eternalizes his personal history in his art, thus magnifying his individual elements into something that can incorporate the significances of the social, the political and the cultural affairs into his unique art-oriented aesthetic space. Absorbing the events that influence his life in exile, Nabokov practices what he claims the magnifying of the small things while breaking down the big things so that all things become equal. Therefore, rather than escaping from the outside world by building a verbal text by art as some critics have asserted, Nabokov cuts the outside events, those social, political and cultural down into smaller things to fit into his custom-made aesthetic space so that these external and public events, though directly influenced his life and family, become the secondary and the subsidiary in his artistic world of past memories which dominate and lead his thread of thoughts and flow of emotions to their predetermined pattern in art. Therefore, the outside world affairs are not an end in themselves. They have further functions in assisting Nabokov to achieve his aesthetic purpose. As it has been discussed in the above, Nabokov intends to write his autobiography in a style that is between fiction and autobiography, fusing both the artistic imagination and the memories of the past events in a conscious way. Then the relationship of the two—the fictional constructions and the memories recollected needs to be specified here so that we can see clearly how Nabokov implements the two, with the former one mainly as the artistic style and the latter mainly as the thematic materials, in his unique autobiography. On the other hand, we can see how Nabokov adapts the cultural issues of his first concerns to his texts of memories.

Viewing from the arrangement of the whole texts of *Speak*, *Memory*, the first chapter, with Nabokov's earliest memories of his past, convey the most metaphysical and epiphanic moments of Nabokov's contemplation of the relationship of his art and memories, his belief in the otherworld pattern in his past memories and the watermark of art hidden in his personal life events. His firm belief in his moving at least toward the right direction by acknowledging a predetermined pattern in the reservoir of remote past, especially the past in Russia, indicates his conscious exertion of his power in artistic construction in order to cope with that fateful and predetermined arrangement which is impersonal, free from man's control. In this chapter, Nabokov sets a tone for his autobiography, declaring the participation of his art in his memory while leading the readers to believe what pleases the author himself is actually the trivialities that recur in a circle, transcending time, repeated in another context many years later but related with each other in a curious way to shock him. The mysterious repetition and pattern in his life events, derived from Nabokov's recollections of his past experiences, is something that Nabokov can not resist and something that makes his life fragments meaningful, artistic and self-conscious. With a special longing of his remote past—his childhood spent in Russia, Nabokov scatters in these first three chapters the most important moments of his life. Though some of them are given more spaces in later chapters of the book to be delivered in a fuller sense, the most significant moments are all touched upon in the beginning. These important moments are repeated in the following chapters of the book and are addressed again in other contexts to reinforce the rhythm of fate. Seen through the whole arrangement of the texts in the chronological order, the repeated trivialities and details in many unexpected places in the following chapters hints at Nabokov's intention of using his most favorite things and most cherished feelings and emotions to transcend time and space and to reconstruct a meaningful associations, thus achieving the eternity and otherworldly aesthetic pattern.

While the past memories of an individual as Nabokov's are recalled in a detached attitude (though this detached attitude results in even more poignancy on the part of the readers), Nabokov handles the cultural issues in the fourteenth chapter—the second chapter from the last before it is too late (the last chapter is mainly about his present state and his remarks toward his wife and his newly-born son and their ready movement toward America). According to Nabokov's recurrent arrangement of his books, he always put the most important epiphanic moments and insightful discoveries near the end of the book when the development of the book have accumulated enough details, effects and emotions. In the fourteenth chapter, he gives his understanding of his exiled life in foreign countries in the context of politics, society, and culture which he only mentions in a sideway in the former chapters and which are only passively and blandly incorporated into his rich and multi-leveled imaginative memories. But in this chapter, he declares in an unambiguous way his attitude toward the life and art in Soviet Russia, the Russian émigré circles, his attitude toward his emigrated country in the continent. It seems that Nabokov, by putting them in the place right before the end of the book, is paying attention all the time to these external affairs that he can not escape from. The only difference is that the larger and more important meaning of these cultural issues judged from the yardstick of the commonsense are here broken down to something of lesser importance, simply to suit the holistic theme and art of Nabokov's memories. When these so-called big issues are confronted with his individual perceptions and sensations of his personal life, they can only be fused into parts and particles of his recollected memories. Losing the original power and significance as they may be when being put into other fictions or other autobiographies, these cultural issues in *Speak*, *Memory* are transformed to serve for Nabokov's holistic aesthetic purpose so as to conform with his art to co-play the harmonious echo. Therefore, the cultural issues are important for Nabokov, but they are important only in a different way from what other novelists usually do. They are important in that they can reinforce Nabokov's unique standing point in his international exile life, airing his voice of independence out of any confinements, free from political and social stresses. With the freedom in his cultural standings, Nabokov achieves the utmost freedom in his art to formulate his sui generis artistic style while trivializing the big issues and enlarging the small things.

In the fourteenth chapter, Nabokov summarizes his life circle through an analogy of a spiral, with each of the three arcs repeating while renovating into something new. This spiral image is further associated by Nabokov with his composition of chess problems in that he devises deliberately the detours and deceptions, taking a roundabout way to achieve his real purpose. Making an analogy between his life in exile and his art in chess, Nabokov consciously constructs his exile in France as some detour and deception in chess to reach his real destination in life toward America. Or it might even be said that his exile life in Germany, France, America and Swiss is his detoured experiences that he has consciously taken only to arrive at his true intention, his real destination—his Russian past. Under the cover of his detailed depictions of the significances and cornerstones in his life, what Nabokov wants to express is his self as deeply pinned in his forever lost Russia, a Russia in his childhood memories reconstructed through artistic imagination. This covering of the real intention through deception and traps is also practiced to its full in Nabokov's art. In this way, his life in exile, his art in chess and his art in fictions are all connected to form a meaningful epiphany that he recognized only many years later. This epiphanic experience delights both himself and his readers to explore further what lies in association with each other between life and art. For Nabokov, the lamp of art pours its light into his life's foolscap, divulging the watermarks in it as patterns that are achieved through the corporation of life and art.

Nabokov's particular way of dealing with his autobiography provides him a space to write his own life in both his fictions and autobiography. When he commented on the portrayal of his relationship with Valentina Shulgina in his first novel *Mary* and in his subsequent autobiography *Speak, Memory*, he said: "I had not consulted *Mashenka* [*Mary*] when writing Chapter twelve of the autobiography more than a quarter of a century later; and now that I have I am fascinated by the fact that despite the superimposed inventions···a headier extract of personal reality is contained in the romantization than in the autobiographer's scrupulously faithful account". (*Mary* xiv) It might be due to that reason that in a discarded introduction to the first version of *Speak, Memory*, *Conclusive Evidence*, he boldly defined his narrative as "the meeting point of an impersonal art form and a very personal life story" (Boyd, *The American Years* 149). Added to this, he indicated in his *Strong Opinion* that a deliberate "distortion of a remembered image may not only enhance its beauty with an added refraction, but provide informative links with earlier or later patches of the past" (*SO* 143). Therefore, like what Galya Diment commented, life, no matter whose, "when imaginatively 'distorted' and 'refracted' rather than slavishly 'recorded' in an unrealistic pursuit of 'objectivity', is much fuller, more dimensional and in the long run, more truly lifelike" (Diment 176). With this belief in mind, Nabokov in his autobiography highlights the cornerstone events, persons and images in his life while constructing them together to form an artistic harmony that can only be achieved through his impersonal art. This harmony is proved by the interlacements of his artistic pursuits, his love of butterflies, chess, his political standings and his understanding of the world outside. In *Speak, Memory*, the details from his life and the insights gained from his life supplement each other with one as the springboard for the other. Both stimulate each other to move to a higher truth in assisting Nabokov to see himself more clearly. Moving in-between the personal history and the artistic strategies, Nabokov presents in a more unambiguous way his life in art.

Highlighting both the cornerstones of life in the past, the miraculous construction and association through art, Nabokov actively selects those life events of him to ingeniously fight against the suppressions brought about by the revolutions in his home country and the poignancies incurred by his lifelong exile. Forming his own artistic space where he can freely roam in any countries proudly and with dignity in a figurative sense, Nabokov exerts his power of being a creative individual, moving in his unique way to counterforce the political, social and cultural marginalization. His strategies involve his evacuation of his past, his elevations of his lifelong hobbies and concerns, his otherworld belief and his artistic imagination of his beloved persons. These personal life events, permeated with strong individual emotions, serve as a strong weapon to expose against the cruelty and terror in human world. And his detached way of presenting them and his parody in dealing with the otherwise excessive romanticism attached to them only make these human emotions truer and more poignant. The highlighting of the personal history, for Nabokov, is in a sense, unavoidable since those cultural influences that are implanted into the very bones of his life can not be neglected when defining his standing point in his fictions and his art.

But the difference is that these personal histories are fictionalized in a way by Nabokov to serve for his deeper understanding of the outside world, assisting his definition of artistic identity and position in a fluctuating world. The voicing of his identity is made possible through the reconstruction of his life that is perceived through an imaginative mind. This well enables Nabokov to creatively obtain a power to fight the negative forces from the society and his exiled life. Wisely transforming his international experiences as something that can set a frame for his home culture and his self, Nabokov reconstructs his recognization of the already unconsciously accepted Russian reality through his distancing of time and space during the exile journey around the world. The boundary between home and world is thus merged in a bridge—an extra-territorial and cross-culture in-between space. It is in this "beyond" that Nabokov asserts his voice and position as a marginalized and displaced diasporic writer. His positive construction of art based on his life stories in *Speak*, *Memory* provides him with wisdom and a platform from which his voice is heard and his deconstruction and reconstruction are accomplished.

I　Past Memories Framed into Pattern of Artistic Consciousness

Nabokov's attitude toward his past is clear in that he divides them into those intellectual ones and those emotional ones. In *Invitation to a Beheading*, he lent his memory of his love affair with Tamara as written in *Speak*, *Memory* to Cincinnatus in his quest toward his no-longer recognizable lover and wife. In *The Real Life of Sebastian Knight*, he assigns many traits of his family members to his characters to deliberately create an effect that merge the fiction and reality. In *The Gift*, He even let Foydor write a biography of his father whose very features are affirmed by Nabokov's mother as shockingly resembling Nabokov's father. In *The Gift*, Nabokov's exile is more detailedly presented through the literary circles of Russian émigrés depicted in the fiction. Assigning from time to time his own life experiences and his own subjective perceptions to his characters, Nabokov is probably directing his art to a way as to have some intimate relationships with his personal life. He might do this due to the following reasons: 1) Taking the past of an individual as the most fascinating things to write about, Nabokov doubts at the meta-narratives of the government and gives affirmation to the narratives of the past of the individual that are re-evoked through the associations of the mind between the past and the present. 2) In assigning to his characters the traits of his own past, Nabokov tests other possibilities of the same traits in fictions so as to relive his own past in a more imaginative way. Positive or negative, these memories in other contexts can resurface in a fictional way so as to guide both the author and the reader to see the patterns that might emerge from them, patterns that seem to be preexisting in a mysterious way before those very life experiences actually take place. 3) Being an artist, Nabokov confuses consciously the fictional and the factual, twisting the factual with his artistic strategies into something unique, something that merges his exile life with his artistic standing point. With the difficulty to tell one from the other, Nabokov successful delivers his idea of the "real". That the fictional versions of reality and the outside world perceived through consciousness is the only truth existed in the world.   Connecting the memories and art and being fascinated by the individual mystery, Nabokov "neither in environment nor in heredity can ··· find the exact instrument that fashioned me, the anonymous roller that pressed upon my life a certain intricate watermark whose unique design becomes visible when the lamp of art is made to shine through life's foolscap" (*SM* 25). Being sensitive to the meanings hidden in his life, Nabokov resorts to his art to distill his insightful understandings of the world around him.

In chapter one of *Speak*, *Memory*, Nabokov talks about the Russia-Japan war in 1904. A friend of his family, General Kuropatkin, came to his house to see his father. Amusing Nabokov who was at the year of five, Kuropatkin played a handful of matches by arranging them on the divan in a horizontal way and said it was the sea in calm weather. Then "he tipped up each pair so as to turn the straight line into a zigzag—and that was 'a stormy sea'" (*SM* 27). When he was about to do a better trick, he was told by his aide-de-camp that he had been ordered from that day to assume supreme command of the Russian Army in the Far East. This is not the end of the memory of this episode. Fifteen years later when Nabokov's father, taking flight from Bolshevik-held St. Petersburg to southern Russia was accosted by an old man to ask for a light, they two recognized each other. The old man is Kuropatkin in disguise whose magic had been fallen through and mislaid and whose armies had vanished. Nabokov points out that what interests him is the evolution of the match theme which repeats itself fifteen years later, only in a different context. While the tricks of the matches were being played, a ruffled reality was also about to be played just as the matches that had been scrambled by Kuropatkin and jumped on the divan as a result of the leaving of his weight. The reality seems to participate in the tricks of Kuropatkin, playing the unfinished trick and continuing the third, "better" trick that he was about to show to the young Nabokov. With the reappearance of the match image fifteen years later, Nabokov draws the connection between these two events that are wide apart in time and space, associating the real with the "unreal" (the "unreal" being Nabokov's infusion of artistic elements into his memory). Transcending time and space, the match theme makes itself meaningful and worthwhile to be mentioned in that it shows how life repeats itself in an unexpected pattern or design and what unreal and mysterious elements that life have incorporated into itself to amaze and amuse one.

　　Immediately after the match theme in the first chapter is demonstrated, Nabokov clearly indicates the core of his book: "the following of such thematic designs through one's life should be, I think, the true purpose of autobiography" (*SM* 27). Dragging and distilling the insightful moments from his past to the utmost, Nabokov interlaces his life and art in the most entangled way in his autobiography. The two moves from one to the other and then back with the sole purpose to defend his identity as an individual and an artist as perceived by himself. The combining of the real and the unreal with a focus on the unreal to regain the loss resulted by time is what Nabokov holds as a belief as his mother did in her life. As an autobiography, *Speak, Memory*, unlike other autobiographies, is extremely conscious of the designs of art that plays in one's life. These designs of art take the form of a meaningful pattern or framework which can well contain the details of his past and his significant life moments of love and creativity. At the same time, this framework or design of art is not a closed one but one that can incorporate both the scientific exactness of the details happened upon the individual and its extended emotions further evoked. Internally, the design works in a self-conscious way, unaffected by the outside forces, forming its own logic. But that does not mean it excludes the social, political and cultural events. It inverts the outside events of the public into its internal logic and discourse and transforms them into functional elements so as to assist the filling of his individual themes in the design. Therefore, the framework that Nabokov consciously designs in his book enables him the utmost expression of his lost childhood Russia in the past, since the "unreal" can compensate for the lost real through preserving and associating the fragments in a meaningful way from the memories. As for the chronological order of the real, it can only be followed in a rough way, giving away to the psychological time of the unreal so that the loss of the past can be regained through breaking of the prison of time.

　　As we have known, the book consists of 15 individual sketches that Nabokov wrote over a time span of 15 years from 1936—1951 with some of them written for other purposes and published in other places. As to the order of these individual ones, Nabokov indicates in the preface of the book that this "order had been established in 1936, at the placing of the cornerstone which already held in its hidden hollow⋯" (*SM* 10) Preexisting even before the writing of the 15 sketches, the framework or the design of the later composed book actually tames each of the fifteen ones to fit into the overall structure. As indicated earlier, the whole structure of the book roughly follows the chronological order while the local parts of the book—the chapters breach the time order. Within the chapters, the prison of time is broken completely as the result of the subjective associations of the mind of the author that conjoins the past, the present and the future. In this way, the basic feature of an autobiography is followed since the life line of the person must be rendered in an autobiography while, at the same time, the freedom of drawing associations through one's memory and imagination is allowed. Even when the rough lifetime order is obeyed in the overall structure, Nabokov's father is seen recurrently in many chapters, giving the whole book a guiding line in theme and tone. Roughly following his life from 1903 to 1940, Nabokov pinpoints the cornerstones in his lifetime in each chapter where he employs cosmic synchronization to start from the core of his life while extending to the other related issues that transcend time and space. Under the construction of artistic strategies, the physical time order compromises with the psychological time order in its merging of the factual and the fictional. Thus the whole book is an autobiography of multi-leveled materials and time-orders, permeated with both the innermost emotions and personal histories that reflect the-then external world affairs.

The psychological time order of art in the book and the physical time order in the depiction of his past life experiences work in the *Speak*, *Memory* both independently and interdependently. This is best exemplified in the theme of Nabokov's father that recurs not only in the level of chapter but in the level of the whole book. Chapter nine is what Nabokov renders as his father's mini-biography. In the five sections of this chapter, Nabokov starts from the matter-of-fact introductory notes on careers of his father as a democratic liberal. Then he moves to talk about the intimate encounters between father and son such as the morning greetings during Nabokov's school days in the second section. The third section is devoted to the prosaic descriptions of the street sceneries on the way to school in St. Petersburg, paving the way for the poignant return from the school after knowing the duel of his father in the last section. In section four, Nabokov turns to his father's arrangement of his Russian education and renders to the reader his father's political belief and his father's passionate political activities. The last section is the longest of the five sections and in it Nabokov expresses his deep love toward his father through his worrying about his father's duel. In this chapter, the time order can be seen breached on the way Nabokov returns from school after knowing from the newspaper that his father might have a duel. On the way back home, Nabokov visualizes his father in the duel ground and extends it to the classic descriptions of the duels ramified in Russian literature along with the real duel that fatally wounded and killed Pushkin in real life. In this way, Nabokov's father's unrealized duel starts to be reflected by literary figures like Pushkin or Lermontov and literary heroes in classic Russian literature. Confusing the line dividing the real and the unreal, Nabokov thus divines his father's image when the factual and the fictional are connected in a dreamy and tragic way while the physical time mingles with the psychological time.

Besides, a series of the most memorable moments that Nabokov shares with his father are recalled on the way back home, including his father's netting for him a rare butterfly, chess played together, words only understood by them two, watching of the tennis games together and "the Pushkin iambics that rolled off his tongue" (*SM* 191). These memorable moments are connected with the things that Nabokov cherishes all his life. And it might be his beloved father who to a large extent guides and directs his desires and passions into these lifelong engagements and activities. The road back home seems to be very long, especially long when there was no car that came to fetch him as usual during "the cold, dreary, incredibly slow drive home in a hired sleigh" (*SM* 189). On the way back home, the details of the duel are visualized by Nabokov and the picture delineated by him only makes him more depressed. In addition, Nabokov ramifies the significant moments that he shared with his father and things happened four or five years ago when his father netted for him "the rare and magnificent female of the Russian Poplar Admirable" (*SM* 192). By the time he went home, "I knew at once there would be no duel, that the challenge had been met by an apology, that all was right" (*SM* 193). But Nabokov does not stop at that. Rather he means to reconstruct the personal history with his artistic strategies. After realizing that his father was safe and sound, he continues to say: "ten years were to pass before a certain night in 1922, at a public lecture in Berlin, when my father shielded the lecturer⋯from the bullets of two Russian Fascists and⋯was fatally shot by the other. But no shadow was cast by that future event upon the bright stairs of our St. Petersburg house" (*SM* 193).

This last passage in chapter nine associates Nabokov's memories of his father who was on the verge of having a duel in St. Petersburg with that in Berlin where he was killed. The thematic echo of the death theme over a lapse of ten years on the part of his father in personal history is further mingled with the afore-mentioned Nabokov's artistic imaginations of the duel scenes as occurred in fictions and his visualization of the possible duel scene of his father. Setting the real in the unreal, Nabokov consciously confuses the two by giving the unreal a more poetic and passionate treatment. Thus the real is hereafter tinged with some divine and mysterious tone without losing its own exactness and precision of personal history. By embedding the most immemorial fragments of the past memories with his father in the sleigh driving back home after school, Nabokov is intending both a literal (personal history) and figurative (artistic epiphany) meaning. In chapter 8 of *Speak*, *Memory*, Nabokov says:

I witness with pleasure the supreme achievement of memory, which is the masterly use it makes of innate harmonies when gathering to its fold the suspended and wandering tonalities of the past. I like to imagine, in consummation and resolution of those jangling chords, something as enduring, in retrospect, as the long table that on summer birthdays and namedays⋯I see the tablecloth and the faces of seated people sharing in the animation of light and shade⋯by the same faculty of impassioned commemoration, of ceaseless return, that makes me always approach that banquet table from the outside, from the depth of the park not from the house—as if the mind, in order to go back thither, had to do so with the silent steps of a prodigal, faint with excitement. (*SM* 171)

In this passage, Nabokov points at the two things that are of major concern of Nabokov's autobiography: 1) The masterly use of memory refers to the artistic selections of the past. The conscious selection from the past events can combine the happenings in the past in a harmonious way so as to achieve artistic pleasure when being recalled. 2) The sensation of ceaseless return that Nabokov cannot resist is the sensation that Nabokov at various life stages obtains through living the past in his mental imagination no matter what real life, however harsh and hard-up, he is leading at the moment. The past memories constructed through his artistic effort remain in his mind as his emotional source to return freely. And the return journey enables Nabokov to rediscover the past that is seen in a new way.

These two points are both demonstrated in his memories of his father. The dead father whom Nabokov returns all the time is his emotional well which offers him power, sensation and delight. The return journey from the outside enables one to see the past from the present sensibility, thus connecting the past with the present. The most memorable memory shared between father and son is best reviewed and fixed by the son when Nabokov the son is on the way back from the outside. Therefore, the longest journey back home with the idea of the possible duel of the father at the back of the mind finalizes and freezes for ever the image of the father in Nabokov's mind. Though the actual duel does not take place, the ceaseless return to the home symbolizes for Nabokov his literal and figurative return to the past that he absorbs power and enlightenment from and thus achieves the happiness through his conscious construction and will. In a detached way, Nabokov discloses his father's death by mentioning it as something attached to the rich and emotional recalling of their happy time together. This only arouses more poignancy on the part of the reader. The duel of his father is here rendered as a sign of fate, a gesture of fate, a premature fateful event that misses but will later be rearranged ten years later by fateful forces. Weaving his father's unrealized duel into part of the scheme of fate in the design of death pattern, Nabokov constructs through his art his memories of his father as something from which the insightful moments arise and guide him toward a carnival experience of art and memory.

The conventional chronological order of an autobiography is broken within the chapters in this book by connecting the fragments of the past through a thematic echo. The thematic connection can associate the life episodes that were wide apart in time and space, thus transcending the conventional time order of the autobiography within the chapter. At the end of the first section of chapter nine, having inherited his father's love of literature, butterflies and chess, Nabokov talks about his father's lifelong passion for opera in which Nabokov is not interested. But that does not stop Nabokov's masterly use of his associations of his memory in terms of theme: "Along this vibrant string a melodious gene that missed me glides through my father from the sixteenth-century organist Wolfgang Graun to my son" (*SM* 179). This connection of musical gene is now constructed by Nabokov from his great-grandfather in the sixteenth century through his father in the first two decades of the twentieth century to his son in the mid-twentieth century and the circle is thus accomplished. The more surprising thing in this chapter is the fact when Nabokov remarks that only recently he read for the first time his father's important collections of articles on criminal law. This collection was given to him by his biographer "Andrew Field who bought it in a secondhand bookshop, on his visit to Russia in 1961" (*SM* 178). Thirty-nine years after the death of his father, the book that Nabokov read for the first time in 1961, was written by his dead father. This book therefore gives one an uncanny feeling that it carries the spirit of his dead father all through the years of his father's absence and recurs after a lapse of almost four decades. The spirit of his father seems to refuse to go and goes on influence his son in an unusual way.

Besides constructing connections through thematic echoes within the chapters, Nabokov also connects the chapters through thematic patterning. In other words, the things discussed in some chapters will be repeatedly touched upon in other chapters as well, only in different contexts. The most prominent one is the theme of his father that occurs in chapter nine, wrought in a mini-biography's framework but recurs in some other chapters as well all through the book, thus forming a unified pattern in the autobiography. For example, the theme of his father appears a couple of times in both the first chapter and the last. In the first chapter, accompanying his description of his father in the attire that is "hard white and gold ··· the resplendent swell of cuirass burning upon his chest and back" (*SM* 20), coming out like the sun was Nabokov's first complete consciousness of the sense of time, of the fact that "I was I and that my parents were my parents" (*SM* 21). With the earliest awakening of his consciousness, Nabokov elucidates his first sensations of his oldest memories and derives great delight and insights from them. One of the memories of his perfect past is his father's being tossed up to the air by the peasants his father had helped to gain rights from the government. Sitting in the room, Nabokov can view through the window his father's alleviations by the hands of the peasants:

　　There, for an instant, the figure of my father in his wind-rippled white summer suit would be displayed, gloriously sprawling in midair, his limbs in a curiously casual attitude, his handsome, imperturbable features turned to the sky. Thrice, to the mighty heave-ho of his invisible tossers, he would fly up in this fashion ··· he would be, on his last and loftiest flight, reclining as if for good ··· like one of those paradisiac personages who comfortably soar, with such a wealth of folds in their garments on the vaulted ceiling of a church while below, one by one, the wax tapers in mortal hands light up to make a swarm of minute flames in the mist of incense, and the priest chants of eternal repose, and funeral lilies conceal the face of whoever lies there, among the swimming lights, in the open coffin. (*SM* 68)

Tossed as "one of those paradisiac personages" and described as "eternal repose", his father is being contrasted with the reference to the "mortal hands". With the split between body and spirit, Nabokov hints that the face in the coffin is the same face that is reclining in the sky and this is the description of Nabokov's father in his coffin with the atmosphere of immortality. Connecting the most vital image in the midair and the most static repose of his father lying in the coffin, Nabokov suggests at the forever living of his father in his heart, as lively as the most impressive sensations that these two images give him.

This idea is further reinforced by Nabokov's letter to his mother: "We shall again see him, in an unexpected but completely natural paradise, in a country where everything is radiance and fineness. He will walk towards us in our common bright eternity⋯Everything will return. In a way that in a certain time the hands of the clock come together again" (qtd. in Alexandrov, *Nabokov's Other-world* 48). In his text, Nabokov does the same thing, regaining the loss through artistic reconstruction of associating his past memories with his thematic pattern that suggests an otherworld sensibility. The pattern constructed around his father develops in chapter two when Nabokov describes an evening in Berlin with his mother. In that evening, he narrates that his mother's words were interrupted by a telephone call. And that day is 28, March, 1922. Without giving further information about that telephone call, Nabokov immediately changes to another topic. But ten pages later, he discloses indirectly that the telephone call must have been about his father's murder when he mentions that his grandfather died on 28, March, 1904, "exactly eighteen years, day for day, before my father" (*SM* 59). This pattern, after its evolution through the chapters, reaches its extended form in the last chapter where Nabokov, directly addressing his wife as "you", expresses his tender love toward his son. In this chapter, he summarizes:

> For every dimension presupposes a medium within which it can act, and if, in the spiral unwinding of things, space warps into something akin to time, and time, in its turn, warps into something akin to thought, then, surely, another dimension follows—a special Space maybe, not the old one, we trust, unless spirals become vicious circles again. (*SM* 301)

The medium that Nabokov employs in his text may seem to be space, time, and a special space that are involved in his metaphor of a spiral form. The space that warps into time is both space and time. And that time warps into thought adds another dimension into time, thus perceived through a self-conscious mind. And this again warps in a new special space incorporating the former space and time. Being one and at the same time being an other, these three phases of the spiral unwinding of things refuses to locate on any single medium, thus enabling Nabokov to freely associate his past sensations in an artistic way, making his cosmic synchronization transcending both time and space. This is how Nabokov treats his memory in art and his art in memory. Here in this part of discussion, we can see that his father's repeated appearance implies a pattern that is constructed in different contexts. The time order of his father's life events is roughly obeyed in the mini-biography in chapter nine. But the realm that Nabokov consciously constructed for his father in his perfect past is an independent space where the best and the happiest moments that he and his father shares or he himself senses. This independent space, housing the most exhilarating memories, is further reinforced and enriched by Nabokov's forever new discoveries and insightful ideas along the time. With the space in time and time in space, Nabokov reaches another special space where his art and his memory units with each other. With artistic constructions and philosophical thinking that he persistently adds, Nabokov formulates a space of a spiral, unwinding things and adding more than one medium to gracefully progress in a way that shocks the world.

II   The Return to the Textual Space in the Past

Nabokov visits and revisits his past in all his works, fictional and non-fictional through many strategic ways. In *Speak, Memory*, he can finally return to his past in an undisguised way, steeping himself deep in the ecstasies that the past memories have brought to him. His return journey to the past in this autobiography thus establishes a textual space through words and discourses. Words and discourses construct a topography where the speaking subject utters his speech and fixes them in written form. This linguistic space, contrived through the fragments of the relics in the remote past, rises from the tomb of history, haunting the author and his present as a ghost. This narrative space obsessively returned by Nabokov houses the most intense emotions, sensations, impressions and ecstasies that Nabokov experienced in his remote childhood in Russia. And his sensual language further uplifts these emotions and sensuousness even into a higher stage. These rich sensuous experiences of the five senses thus bring the body to the fore and the excesses of the body transform Nabokov into that past space where things become intimate again via Nabokov's greatest physical details. The sensuous experiences of the body restore a closer relationship with things in the textual space of the past that Nabokov reinvented. The "speculary self" (Certeau, *Heterologies* 56) in the past haunts the "social self" in the present, offering great attractions and appeals to him so that Nabokov can temporarily exile himself from the present reality into the "unreal" realm through a space of text of words and discourses. This "unreal" realm is actually the most real for Nabokov since the things in the past in a child's eyes are less contaminated by the symbolic order of the grow-up's world.

Things of the past presented by Nabokov are preserved to their most original forms through Nabokov's familiar but strangely beautiful words, making great effort to reduce the distance between word and thing. The status of that realm seems to struggle to become what Lacan call the "mirror stage" of a child. In this stage, identifying himself with the mother, the child enjoys a whole sense of himself while maintaining the most natural connection with the things around him. The child mirrors himself in his mother and sees his own reflections in the mother. But the child loses his identification with his mother when he learns the word "mother". The word "mother" deprives the child of his identification with the mother and separates the child from his identified self—the mother. From that time on, the child's desire for the mother in his later life stage can never be satisfied and is thus plunged into a lack-of being stage—the "Symbolic Order". Being introduced into language, the child represses his desire for the identification with mother and all his efforts to regain for that object he desires can only aim for the "other". By pursuing word/signifier, the child grows up to hope to fill the blank left by the initial loss of identification with the mother. However, by naming, one sacrifices the object, since the presence of the sign/word is the absence of the signified /thing.

Nabokov treats his past as something eternalized by his memory and unharassed by the change of time and space. This understanding of the past provides Nabokov with the perfect realm where things there maintain the initial connections with themselves, free from being deprived of the signified by the signifiers/words. The term— "perfect past" that Nabokov originally uses as the title of his first chapter, originally as a sketch, discloses his intention that his past exists for him as things rather than as words. The signified are always there, free from the eliminations by the signifiers that always substitute the signified/things. Nabokov tends to show that these things are not named but acted out. And the things happened there in the past are speech-acts. What appeals to Nabokov in this realm of the past is the security and identification that he can never hope to find in the chain of signifiers that he has pursued in the world of language and the "symbolic order". By designating the past with such a status, Nabokov distinguishes his past, especially the remote past from his present. By placing the past and present at two extremes, Nabokov's space of text is established. His return journey to the past offers him a means to desire for that lost object since the past depicted by him seems to be endowed with a divinity of natural harmony where things are most real and people maintains relationship with the undifferentiated matter of natural existence. Alienated from the initial contact with the natural existence and suffered the loss of his identification with his mother as Lacan's idea shows to us, Nabokov cannot resist the call from the wild and returns again and again to the past so as to offset the torture of the lack-of-being in the present real life in hope of the retrieval of the lost object. The desire for object is only compensated by a chain of signifiers to replace the whole we always miss. But it can only be done by the part. As John Rivkin says "the small "o" other or initial object becomes the large "O" Other of the symbolic unconscious" (Rivkin 394). The chain of signifiers to forever reach the "mother" or initial connection with the natural existence can only refer to the "Other".

The absence of the object itself evokes Nabokov to construct the textual space with multiplications of words to fill in the blank left. These signifiers used can only be the signifiers of the "Other". Therefore, the textual space is also the textual space of the other. The speaking self, separated from itself by language, is impossible to regain its whole self. The only way to release the torture of the desire for its own self is to obsessively speak of the signifiers which can only refer to the other in order to reach a hypothesized self. In Nabokov's case, the other that he used to approach the self—the "I" is seen always located in his past life experience and it seems that only these signifiers of the other in the locus of the past can offer a possibility or a precondition for the desire of the self and are thus nearer to his "specularly self" than any other in terms of infinitely approaching the self. By going back to the past in hope of unifying with the self, the text has to resort to the other to obtain that hypothesized self. Therefore, the presence of the other denotes the desire for the self, that absent self. In this way, Nabokov's textual space is both a space of narrative and at the same time, the space of the other. It is the same with the formerly discussed books of Nabokov. Nabokov, by setting a locus of fantasy and a locus of metafiction respectively in *Invitation to a Beheading* and *The Real Life of Sebastian Knight*, creates the doublings of the protagonists—the speaking "I" to illustrate his own self in a negative way—in the way that is through the other. By saying "I am not that", Nabokov establishes topography of different discourses on various levels to maintain a detached distance from the self that he wants to approach. The proliferations of "I am not that" in a best way multiplies the signifiers of the signified, giving birth to a numerous amount of words/signifiers to fill in the blank of the black hole/signified that always recedes at the approaches of these signifiers of the other.

In this self-consciously created space of the other, Nabokov repeatedly stresses the fateful power existed in his life experiences of the past. Apart from giving his life in the past an artistic imagination, the text seems to have an invisible hand to manipulate the fragments of Nabokov's life in a predestined way. This mysticism lurking in some corners of the depictions of his life in the past transports the narrative with reason and ration into the text with irrational, unknowable elements that are constantly working there. For this, Nabokov desires and acclaims each time after having presented the factual narrative in a most detailed and private way. The effects accumulated through the deliverance of the physical details always can bring him to a spiritual enlightenment, transporting him from the present social order to another status where ecstasies and willed happiness reign. This realm of happiness is the otherworld, the watermark of Nabokov's life events, seen only through the light of imagination and artistic creativity. The imagination of the past event, i. e. the combination of art and memory transports Nabokov into a state where word and thing are one and the same and the self that one desires to have identification is obtained. Nabokov strives to reach the otherworld in the above discussed two books through the death or damnation of the body of the protagonists. The otherworld that Cincinnatus and Sebastian Knight strive for is reached in sacrifice of the body. In *Speak*, *Memory*, Nabokov, through the spiritual guidance of the deaths of his father and his family members, reach in a detoured way that ecstasy of joining with the self. Through the speeches of his speaking subject "I" in his autobiography, Nabokov utters multiplications of signifiers of the other to reach that hypothesized self.

Therefore, the otherworld that refers to the other side of the boundary between life and death in Russian transports both Nabokov and his protagonists in his autobiography and fictions in hope of having the chance of a glimpse at the self that is forever lost at the dawn of consciousness and language. It can only be paid off through the denunciation of the body so as to return to that primary state of connection with "I" . Death that allows one to return to that primary link with the object is here simulated through stepping into the soul of the dead family members to borrow a perspective that is otherwise impossible for the living in the mundane world. To enter the soul of the late beloved, Nabokov needs language to utter that soul or desires of identification with it. However, the words uttered are always the signifiers of the other, not the original thing itself since word takes the place of the thing and word always refers to part of the whole or simply misses the target. With this fundamental gap between word and thing, Nabokov establishes the textual space that sets the past and present, the dead and the living, the individual and commonsense into two extremes. The process of the development of the two extremities gives birth to the matrix of fictional descriptions which constitutes the novel itself. In this textual space, the discourse of the other is given utmost deliverance, enabling it to convey the object desired. Therefore, pinned in such an absolute loss of the object, Nabokov is fully aware that the discourse of the other is the only medium or possibility to reach his otherworld where things have their original and natural connections with their existences. In this sense, "I" is the other. And the textual space of the autobiography—*Speak*, *Memory* is both the space of narration of self and space of the other. The two senses take place simultaneously. If Nabokov speaks himself through the doubling of Cincinnatus in the locus of a fantasy in *Invitation to a Beheading* and through the doubling of Sebastian Knight in the locus of metafiction in *The Real Life of Sebastian Knight*, he, in *Speak*, *Memory*, is attempting to give himself a psychological analysis of the self to see if there are some bones of the past that are latent but can be dug up in identifying himself in a more enlightening way. Then posited in the context of the textual space of the other, the otherworld that Nabokov desires embodies all the attempts that one, who is absorbed into the symbolic order, desires of going back to that "specu-lary self" in "mirror stage".

Therefore, the otherworld in Nabokov's art is something that is consciously constructed by him so as to address his individuality and uniqueness to remain aloof away from the public consciousness while at the same time demonstrating his desire of the "real" or "I". But he is careful enough not to name it. He is fully aware that the very naming of the otherworld deprives the thing of itself and is doomed to refer to the other. What we read in his texts instead is his multipli-cations of the signifiers of the other to refer to the otherworld, including his neg-ative presentations of his depictions of the otherworld—what is not other-world. He keeps addressing the readers that what he means is something else, something that is both this and that and some others. It is not this and not that and it is something more. These infinite multiplications of words and discourses of the signifiers negate themselves but at the same time combine with each other so as to allow more words and discourses to be added for that infinitely receding signified—the otherworld in Nabokov's sense. The textual space itself is open, ready to include more signifiers while the urge to the otherworld/signified consti-tutes the major engine to drive the words and discourses to speed into that terra incognita for ecstasy and happiness. The inner power of Nabokov's text to move forever to the unknown territory can thus be seen as originating from the obsessive urge to the space of the past which most likely offers the possibility of transporting him to his identification with the object. This possibility of identification with "I" is presumably realized in discursive level of the other through the speech of the speaking "I". Though the speech can not fully reach the object, it can at least provide Nabokov with signifiers of the other to reach that imagined signified. Therefore, Nabokov's speaking "I" speaks the discourse of the other to realize his desire of the "I" in the space of the past imagined. In addition, the "I" that Nabokov is eager to utter is most mystically disguised in his pursuit of words for expressing his unknown territory—the otherworld. His "somewhere else" or "something else" repeated in the book best illustrates the fact that in some sense his otherworld means both a special space and a special thing/signified. Therefore, the otherworld is identified with his pursuit of self—the speaking "I" that speaks through the ghost of history. The only difference of the otherworld and the speaking "I" in the aspect discussed above is that the otherworld provides both a locus/space and an utterance for the speaking "I" to reside and to be disguised.

The text in *Speak, Memory* sets up a textual space by establishing the discourses that negate the discourses of the common sense, the traditional and the modern. Like what Certeau sees Montaigne's "Of Cannibals", here I would like to see the textual space as established through Nabokov's discourses of negation of the accepted discourses of the societies. In the first chapter, Nabokov starts the book by saying:

> Common sense tells us that our existence is but a brief crack of light between two eternities of darkness···Nature expects a full-grown man to accept the two black voids, fore and aft, as stolidly as he accepts the extraordinary visions in between. Imagination, the supreme delight of the immortal and the immature, should be limited. In order to enjoy life, we should not enjoy it too much···I rebel against this state of affairs. I feel the urge to take my rebellion outside and picket nature. (*SM* 19—20)

Common sense tells us that one should live a life with ration and routine so as to enjoy life in an utmost way. Any irrational dreams and imagination beyond the solid living on earth is regarded as incurring unnecessary troubles and unpractical emotional strife that may disturb a peaceful and efficient mind. Never giving a thought to look outside the light of life at the darkness beyond, man fools themselves and lives a self-deceptive and self-content life of an egoist. For Nabokov, it is the acceptance of the common sense ideas of the world without referring to the two sides of life that confines people in a time prison and restricts their imaginative understanding of their individuality. Negating the common sense discourse of life as a brief crack and the darkness before and after life as the two eternities, Nabokov journeys back to his past life which offers a possibility of transcending time that confines man within his life boundaries to view the possible impact that might be made by the two eternities upon our life itself. Turning the past as a media to gain further perspectives to reflect back on human life, Nabokov demonstrates his making "colossal efforts to distinguish the faintest of personal glimmers in the impersonal darkness on both sides of my life" (*SM* 20). Distancing his discourse from the unimaginative discourse of the common sense, Nabokov makes his past occupy in a sweeping way his autobiography by transcending life out of the time-space confinement in hope of gaining another new perspective.

Nabokov also distances his discourse from the traditional discourse of literature: the genre of the autobiography. In the first chapter, he declares that the thematic designs through one's life should be the true purpose of autobiography. By emphasizing the role of art played in his book, Nabokov stands aloof from the ordinary autobiographies through the fateful power of his otherworld theme. The otherworld theme connects and associates the seemingly unrelated fragments and events in his life in the past and emerges after his recollection as showing him an amazing coincidence and evoking pattern that seem to be preexistent and divine in its power of arranging life for the moral people. Through these patterns, Nabokov sees an invisible authority guiding his life and makes its appearance through traces that need to be reconstructed through recollection and reconstruction. Through the journey back to the past, Nabokov gains artistic delight that he might not have imagined if he was amid the events of the past himself and thus enjoys the happiness that he wills in a conscious way to reorganize his life fragments through his artistic reconstruction. The joy is realized by his demonstration of his particular practice of "cosmic synchronization" that is based on a philosopher's idea and that co-places the things together regardless of the time element. This is also his discourse that is against the commonly practiced chronological discourse in autobiography. In addition, he adds his lifelong concern to the butterflies and moths into his discourses. The scientific discourses about his professional knowledge on them gains his autobiography another dimension of exactness and meticulousness.

While standing away from the traditional discourses of the genre of autobiography, Nabokov is also particular in demonstrating his critical view of literature in a general way by pinpointing the literary discourses of Soviet Russia back in his homeland and his views on literary circles in the continent. Being ironic against those trendy reviews of literature and those general and flat criticisms of hacks and editors, he clears his discourses away from those social novels, fictions of ideas and works of fuzzy emotions. Against the discourses of modern culture, Nabokov upholds a discourse that pays attention to the individual perception of the world and the details that he uses to depict the man and the things in the world pay respect to the uniqueness of each individual. This is not only an aesthetic discourse but also an ethic discourse. The attention paid to humanity in Nabokov's discourses demonstrates his political position of fighting against the terrorism and cruelty of the world politics.   In his émigré countries of the European continent, he indicates that the Russian émigré writing circle in Europe is vital in life and adds color and imagination to the dull writing circle of their emigrant countries to the extent that "we ignored them the way as arrogant or very stupid invader ignores a formless and faceless mass of natives" (SM 276). Depicting his past life around some major figures in his life and absorbing the outside world affairs into his personal historical discourses, Nabokov shows his profound feelings toward them. By magnifying his emotion and consciousness to the utmost and reducing the historical affairs into trifles, Nabokov fights against the modern discourse of culture in his unique way so as to focus on the persons and

things that weave an otherworld pattern in an individual's life. By setting the negative discourses against other possible ones, Nabokov establishes topology of
textual space for the utterance of the other or the speaking "I".

The three reference points that Nabokov sets to show his attitudes build the
layers of the space of his narrative and at the same time the space of the other. The series of three discourses become disconnected with each other because
there is a distance intervening between them. Rising from these three criteria,
Nabokov demonstrates his unique points that are different from each one of
them. The distance that Nabokov sets between his discourses and the generally
accepted ones lay bare the disconnections between Nabokov's and the public's as
well as the disconnections in between the three publicly accepted ones. Only
when the combination of the three is added with what Nabokov demonstrates as
his own peculiar discourses, the textual locus of the book is established. Only
when this combination struggles to move to the impossible center point of the
conjunction of those elements can the saying of the thing be realized. As noted by
Certeau, the series of the discourses of the other are "structured as a written
discourse: the written text, a spatial dissemination of elements destined for an
impossible symbolization, dooms the unity it aims for (the thing, or meaning),
as well as the unity it presupposes (the speaker), to inaccessible (by the very
fact of the exteriority of the graphs to one another)" (Certeau, *Heterologies*
72). In this space of the narrative, Nabokov demonstrates his utterances in a
way that can multiply more signifiers of the other so as to reach the forever receding signified that he pursues all his life. Lacan reiterates that " 'there is a
One' " which is always the Other. On condition that one 'never have recourse to
any substance' nor to 'any being,' 'speaking brings God' and 'as long as
something will speak, the hypothesis God will be there'" (Certeau, *Heterologies* 59).

For Nabokov, the same is true. In the textual space that he all the way establishes as something that is rebelling against the commonly accepted ones, he
prepares for himself wisely a unique space for slipping toward his otherworld locus where a unique perspective that transcends the life and time-space of this
world can be obtained. His desire of the happiness of the otherworld thus is

brought out through the recollections of the absent relics explored by a present consciousness. Along with the past fragments recalled are a Nabokov that shares the same aura and identity with the lost things. In recalling the past, the present Nabokov transforms the lost things into something that is free from time and space, something mystic and eternal. At the same time, in the process of the recalling, he transports this divinity and myth that he confers to the things into his self in that long-lost Russian home. According to Along with reconstructing the lost things, Nabokov consciously reconstructs his self through the work which is his speech that exercises the desire. The desire for identification with his self back in Russia before the exile becomes something that has been lost forever but can be reconstructed through his art after a lapse of a couple of decades, distanced at a far-away space. The reconstructed images of his past life carry with them Nabokov's emotions and longings toward the absence of the thing in his memory. The presence of the words substitutes the absence of the thing and hopes to revive a series of signifiers of the other to approach a hypothesized signified. As long as the words are there, the hypothesized signified is there.

III　The Self-analysis of the Speaking "I"

As an autobiography, *Speak, Memory* belongs to the genre that incorporates both the personal history of a given person and the literary elements of fiction. According to Philippe Lejeune as quoted in Michael de Certeau's book, "the autobiographical genre is grounded not on the text itself, but on the conjunction between the author named by the text and his effective social place" (Certeau, *Heterologies* 32). In his remarks, there involves a combination of two elements: a personal history realized by the autobiographical fiction and a public domain of that person evaluated by an institutional parameter. Viewed from Certeau's perspective provided in his analysis of history and literature as well as Freudian novels, history is related to the real, the reality so as to maintain its authority of verisimilitude while literature such as poems needs "nothing" in order for one to give credit to it. In this sense, the poem has no reality to support. It relies on belief that is born out of a void and is the creator of a void. In a different way, historical discourses need legitimization and institution from the outside society to give it authority to make people believe. Certeau, in his analysis of Freudian novel, gives a clearer discussion of the two elements combined in Freud's works that incorporate both the scientific discourse and poetic/literary ones. As both a psychoanalytic scientist and a writer of literary works, Freud, in his psychoanalytic works, addresses these two strategies to make clear his theory and practice.

According to Certeau, Freud's work or psychoanalytical works contain two very different texts: one gives theory and the other expounds upon it like the knowledge of the teacher (Certeau, *Heterologies* 28). For these two texts,

> Theory insists on the "supposed" knowledge of the analyst which refers back to "nothing" of knowledge and to the demystifying reciprocity in the relationship of one to another. But the practice is often dependent on the accredited "knowledge" of the affiliation and on the proper name of the institution. " (Certeau, *Heterologies* 28)

In the theoretical aspect, Freud's theory itself is subject to the transformations and deformations since it refers back to "nothing" of knowledge. But in the practical analysis of the cases of patients, it is required that the "supposed" knowledge that refers back actually to "nothing" should be legitimized as institutions to make them credible so as to be didactic in expounding on them. Being fully aware of this instability, Freud is seen by Certeau as maneuvering "between the 'nothing' of writing and the 'authority' that the institution furnishes the text" (Certeau, *Heterologies* 33). Being "authorized by its adherence to the events which it is believed to explicate or to signify," (Certeau, *Heterologies* 32) the theoretical text of Freud gains the authority through adopting the scientific discourse for its power of institutization while sticking to the nothingness of the writing which from the very beginning is the unreal content inside the real scientific framework of the institution. The same applies to Nabokov's texts. As we know, in *Speak, Memory* as well as in his other works, Nabokov's love of natural sciences and his great wonder at the mimicry of nature develop themselves in his literary discourses of his works as his lifelong passion for butterfly collecting, including his early passion for the naming of a new species and his scientific studying of the particular organ of the butterflies. We also know that he shows contempt to those fuzzy poems that are overwhelmed with empty passions and foggy emotions but lack of any precisions and knowledge towards the objects themselves described in those romantic poems.

In *Speak, Memory*, Nabokov's combination of his two roles deserves our attention. On the one hand, he is the recorder of his family histories and the family makeup. For this, according to Philippe Lejeune's remarks in another field, the autobiographical genre is grounded not on the text itself, but on the conjunction between the author named by the text and his effective social place. In Certeau's words, it can be explained as the idea that the accreditation of the author by his historical place generates the legitimation of the text by its referent" (Certeau, *Heterologies* 32) His role as a member of a scientific profession or academic association "brings to his discourses a double strength and this strength is represented within the discourses by the supposed link between the utterance and the facts to which it refers…Social credentials play a decisive role in the definition of the discourse's status" (Certeau, *Heterologies* 32) Therefore, in this sense, one does not believe in the writing but in the institutions that legitimatize the authority of the discourses. Here, the text's obedient attitude toward the common facts that refer to the norms of a community shows the text's "conformity" to the facts. Seen from this perspective, the life history of Nabokov's aristocratic nobility unavoidably relies on the outside reality of his family and historical documents and records are used to support and validify their family reality so as to add authority to them. Here his conformity to the norms of reality gains for his discourse legitimization and credibility and it is the institution that solidifies its framework of the real. In addition, his emphasis on his passion towards moths and butterflies results in a scientific description of the minute details of the inside out of the insects.

In Nabokov's case, his information on butterfly excludes any unprofessional, fuzzy and dallying of the subject. The authority that Nabokov assigns to his knowledge painstakingly gained through great curiosity and great dedication does not allow any light-hearted remarks and comments. Although Nabokov dreams of pursuing a particular species of butterfly to distinguish himself from the other scientists in his early years to be unique and different, he unavoidably resorts to the scientific parameters to institutionize his knowledge in his *Speak*, *Memory* and other fictional and non-fictional works. Like Freud's texts, it is his very scientific discourses that provide a framework of the real, enabling the unreal to be carried out within. This framework is institutionized and it lends authority and credulity to his poetic discourses of his enlightenments, epiphanies, the otherworld sensibility that refer back to "nothing" of knowledge which is born of a void and creator of a void. In this way, the scientific discourses that are used in the field of butterflies privilege Nabokov with a professional knowledge that he can safely rely on to contain his imaginative literary discourse of "nothing". The details and precisions that Nabokov is good at in treating the substantial things serve the same purpose of making the insubstantial things authoritative by establishing a connection with the real. His reference to the reality that is delineated almost in a scientific way makes his works stand out as unique and exact with institutionized knowledge to which the other novelists have no access. His precise representation of the outside reality, the real and professional knowledge on certain scientific field lend both authority and a form or a framework of the real to his writing.

On the other hand, Nabokov is a writer who aims at evoking beauty and new perspective from his imaginary construction of art. His poetic discourses of his personal history deprive the history of its presence and use words to fill the blank of that loss of the past. Thus the writing "takes the place of" history and constructs a discourse that relies on belief rather than on institution since there is no outside reference for the writing to refer to. In this way, the writing that is originally excluded from the history takes history's place, smearing off its traces and establishing a functional stage on which it asserts itself. In *Speak*, *Memory*, since Nabokov constructs it as something between autobiography and fiction, his writing in this fictionalized autobiography in a way needs not to be validified because "there need exist nothing for one to believe in it" (Certeau, *Heterologies* 31). Mallarme speaks of "belief" and holds that believing attaches writing to "nothing" . Since the poetic writing supports no reality and it is originated no longer in being, it is the writing of nothing. Being put within the framework of the real, his most cherished "real" , which is unreal in other people's view——the lost past that is imagined and constructed out of a nothing—a void, obtains both belief of nothing and substantial authority borrowed from his "scientific discourses" . The scientific discourse helps the text to gain a dimension of real in its role of offering precise knowledge on subjects related to institutions. However, there is one thing that should be noted. Nabokov's precise knowledge as provided on the subject of butterflies, moths, and mimicry in nature is closely related to his poetic discourse of "nothing" . To put in another way, because of Nabokov's artistic fusions of various elements in his life, the scientific subjects are elevated to the imaginative level and become the basis from which he can spring up to his epiphanic otherworld "nothingness". This extension of the exact details from the scientific discourse to his poetic narrations/discourses of the objects and scenes in his past memories accounts partly for the reason why Nabokov's texts are convincingly definitive and at the same time imaginatively poetic and divine. Therefore, *Speak, Memory* can be seen as a work with a locus of the real holding the utterance of the unreal or Nabokovian "real" . It is these two that have combined to produce a mixed ambivalence and exactness.

However, what is realized through his impersonal artistic strategies of the scientific and poetic discourses is a self-analysis of Nabokov's personal history. For this, Nabokov, consciously and unconsciously, seeks to settle down something that concerns his artistic position, exile and cultural standings so as to escape some possible deviations that might be incurred by his works and life and might be misunderstood by the public in the future. With the consciousness of explaining the present "I" through the past "I" and elucidating the past "I" at a distance both in time and space, Nabokov joins his past "I" *and* his present "I" creatively in the process of self-exploration in order that the two can inter-elucidate each other. Like a patient in a psychoanalytic treatment, Nabokov journeys consciously back to his past to seek for some possible explanations or knowledge for his present self—a self that is haunted by the things lost. Once

this conscious process starts, the suppressed emerges and returns to fight for itself to be acknowledged in a way that is out of Nabokov's expectation. As the
heart of the process that psychoanalysis is based on, the return of the repressed
indicates that "consciousness is both the deceptive *mask* and the operative *trace*
of events that organize the present" (Certeau, *Heterologies* 3). In this case,
the overt and the hidden combine to lead the process into a new discovered "I"
that is not only reconstructed but is originated from the repressed. Therefore,
there is a possibility that the self-analysis unveils the true things underneath the
deceptive consciousness though the consciousness is actively evoked by Nabokov.

Nabokov in *Speak, Memory* addresses his wife Vera as "you" and in some
points of his personal history he directly speaks to her as if she were an audience
to hear his speech. This is very much like what a psychoanalyst does in treating
his patient. In the context of psychoanalytical case, the analysand speaks to the
analyst his history. In this process, the analysand is required to elaborate on the
things that are presumably connected with his madness or obsessions. Facing the
analyst, the analysand presumes that the analyst obtains the knowledge that can
cure his obsessions and madness. Therefore, he makes efforts to recollect and
reconstruct the stories of his personal history of his past and whatever he regards
that are related to his obsession. With this process, the matrix of his fictional
rendering of his history is thus formed. And it is during this process that he
seems to rediscover something new from his past and it seems that the old bone
of his past returns to bite him and asks for re-cognition. This uncanny feeling
that the unfamiliar turns out to be the familiar repressed at some critical moments
of one's life is what Freud terms as the return of the suppressed. The speech thus
uttered by the analysand constitutes his discovery of some "new" elements that
are supposed to be non-existent or have nothing to do with the engaged issue and
in this way meets the knowledge that is supposed to be held by the analyst. Different from the psychoanalytic treatment of the evocation of the analyst of
the analysand, Nabokov's is a self-imposed one with his strong determination of
streaming things about his life-concerns out in a clear way. He sets Vera as his
assumed audience and himself as a person who seeks to reconstruct the self

through a journey back. In speaking to an audience in a confessional way, Nabokov projects outward his innermost things through verbal discourses. In this way, he can better see his self that is objectified out in concrete metaphors, images and symbols. Traveling to the past, the present self is having a dialogue with its past self hidden in deep entangles with history, private and public. In this case, a self-assumed analysis with very strong self-consciousness actually takes place.

For Nabokov, his emphasis on the active reference to one's history and to one's obsessive desire for certain objects or things partly goes as something ironic against Freud's analysis of the child's desire of his mother. For Freud, man's desires and obsessions come from the unconscious libido that drives him to act accordingly. Being out of control of the rational man, the unconscious desires make their appearance in one's works and behaviors in an opaque way. Writing for Freud is an exercise of desires that offers an outlet in the textual space of the dream-work for the writer to achieve the bliss since one is not expected to fulfill and satisfy in reality. On the issue of the past and personal history, Freud indicates clearly in his *The Uncanny* that the unheimlich comes from the heimlich because it is the repression of the desires of the early life that return. The uncanny feeling that the unfamiliar actually comes from the familiar discloses the inverted desires of the individual and accounts for the reason of some strange obsessions in the later stage of the man. As a result, the speaking "I" of the present is deeply and sophisticatedly entangled with the "I" in Russia, in England, in Berlin, in Paris, in America and even in Swiss. Being deeply buried in different stages of the "I", the speaking "I" seeks to incorporate them all into its system to formulate them in a meaningful and thought-provoking way. On the one hand, the various known parts of the "I" can remind the speaking subject of the relationships among themselves so as to coalesce a meaningful theme from them while evoking the lost and unknown parts of "I" that are hidden but wait to be excavated in the process of recalling the strong impressions that the past events made on the mind. On the other hand, the explosion of the various versions of the speaking "I" as related to one event or theme fulfills the task of conjoining the speaking "I" with the otherworld both in structure and in utterance. The juxtapositions of various fragments of the past, present and future inter-refer each other with one element or theme as a coalescing structural motif while radiating toward the remotest and cultivating the imagination to the utmost. Breaking the time and space confinement of this world and being guided by a power that connects all the fragments in a preexistent way, the otherworld space is thus formulated for the speaking "I" to have a clearer view of itself.

For example, the four years of diligent retrieval of his Russian language and construction of Russian world in Cambridge is recalled by the present "I" as supplying "not only the casual frame, but also the very colors and inner rhythms for my very special Russian thoughts" (*SM* 269). The "I" that was about to leave Cambridge suddenly felt that "something in me was as naturally in contact with my immediate surroundings as it was with my Russian past, and this state of harmony had been reached at the very moment that the careful reconstruction of my artificial but beautifully exact Russian world had been at last completed" (*SM* 270). In recalling, the "I" that was trying everything to avoid the culture in England is replaced by the "I" that finds out it has unconsciously practiced the transformation of Russian past into Cambridge's time-space, reliving in a creative way Russian past in another environment. From the perspective of the present "I", the Cambridge environment that Nabokov had stayed now plays a symphony with his Russian past. Transporting the various environments into the identifying shadows of his Russian past, the present "I" comes to the awakening of his former unconscious transformation and then later conscious transplantation of his Russian past in different time-space. Thus he is seen approaching nearer his hypothesized "I" by adding another version of signifiers of the other. The combinations of the other/utterances of "I" might bring him nearer to his true self.

Nabokov's conscious self-analysis also derives from his "burdens" of romantic love. He admits that the girls that linger in his life in Russia and the sceneries that arouse his feelings about them all suppress him when he did not know how to find an outlet to release. The impressions and echoes resulted from them refuse to go away from his present life before they are let out through proper ways. For these, he now finds art as a useful means to "transform them into something that can be turned over to the reader in printed characters to have him cope with the blessed shiver" (*SM* 212). Enlarging and extending his personal emotional burdens into his impersonal art, Nabokov releases the recurrent returns of his personal past out of his overwhelming well of emotions into art. The shivering that the readers are aroused by his poetic discourses is what Nabokov aims at. The shivering shared between the writer and the reader betrays Nabokov's concern toward the things and people in his past and his conscious intentions of deviating them to larger outlets. From this, we can see two Nabo kovs: one is deeply infiltrated in his past and the other is calmly combing the accumulated emotions in an impersonal way, adding a rational dimension into it. At the same time, one is the unconscious self that is on the verge of slipping into the unconscious realm of the repressed and the other is the conscious artistic self controlling the direction, the tone and the utterance of the discourses. The different versions of the self with the help of memory come as a delight for Nabokov in enjoying sharing them with the readers while formulating the series into self-conscious shadows of the signified that is absent.

In his chapter of butterfly, Nabokov uses butterfly as his structuring theme to connect the "I" in different stages in terms of hunting butterfly. As a symbol that carries Nabokov's many concerns, butterfly arouses in his life the most sensational and epiphanic delights: 1) The subject of the butterfly incorporates Nabokov's love of his father who has left the unforgettable episodes and intimate moments shared between father and son in Nabokov's memory. 2) Butterfly, treated as a professional life-long interest, evokes Nabokov to draw them out in exact and precise verbal discourses and thus transforms them from the image into the words. This inspires him to write in an exact way in depicting his characters, his sensations of life and memories of the past. It is now his practice of the magnifying of the trivialities. 3) The non-utilitarian delight that Nabokov obtains from the mimicry of the butterflies as a typical insect of nature indicates his major concern of art—that is, art and nature are "both a form of magic…a game of intricate enchantment and deception" (*SM* 125). 4) Butterfly carries another symbolic dimension as an insect that undergoes a stage of new birth. The life after death is something that Nabokov has faith in and it is his major way of look ing at the life of this world from the two dark abysses that breaks the time prison of the mortals. 5) Butterfly can transport Nabokov to a special space, a place that contains his most cherished things in the world. The mythic ecstasy aroused by "rare butterflies and their food plants" (*SM* 139) suggests the otherworld that lies behind:

> This is ecstasy, and behind the ecstasy is something else, which is hard to explain. It is like a momentary vacuum into which rushes all that I love. A sense of oneness with sun and stone. A thrill of gratitude to whom it may concern——to the contrapuntal genius of human fate or to tender ghosts humoring a lucky mortal. (*SM* 139)

In this special space, butterflies serve as a medium through which Nabokov is transported to the otherworld ecstasy where the self experiences "the highest enjoyment of timelessness" (*SM* 139). Freeing itself from the unbreakable wall of the earthly life, the self enters the otherworld realm through his recalling of the butterflies. Impersonalized by the conscious efforts of the fusion of the self, the butterfly and the otherworld, Nabokov is at the same time showing his repressed desires of the unnamable—something that belongs to a timeless consciousness. No longer a mere insect, butterfly incorporates into itself the most cherished emotions and ideas of Nabokov and thus in a way reflects Nabokov's self from another dimension.

Nabokov's desire for the otherworld where he can express his speaking "I" in a disguised way leads him to strive for the timeless consciousness that can break the time sphere and achieve the perspective to see life from both two sides of life. To strive for the almost impossible otherworld perception and power, Nabokov designs in each chapter of *Speak, Memory* a different theme. In each one of the theme, Nabokov establishes first a space of the other where the past things are lost but the words are there. The words that substitute the absent things further evoke more words of the other to fill the forever receding blank. The process of seeking the metaphors, images, and analogies to fill the hole forms a matrix of fictional words and discourses that is the fiction it-

self. While providing an outlet for the writer to relieve the burden of the repressed off him, the carnival of signifiers of the other also brings the writer to
the delight and happiness of the otherworld. Here Nabokov's concerns are as follows: 1) by aiming at his personal history, he explores his self that is lost and
now the hypothesized self is regained through words. 2) The many themes that
he centers on in different chapters combine to play a chord of the speaking "I"
since these themes all entangle deeply with each other and with the self. 3) The
self-conscious construction of the textual space of the other shows Nabokov's determination of his positive reshaping of his past to break off the closed circuit of
time so as to gain the perception of the dead—another dimension and side of
life. 4) In the process of the revelation of the self, his scientific discourses that
is used in his professional knowledge of this world's reality helps him to define in
a way his poetic discourses of the otherworld. The otherworld offers Nabokov a
space where he can drown himself in his ecstasy of his unified self.

IV   The Practice and Creation of the Self in Exile

Nabokov's *Speak, Memory* is declared to be something between autobiography and fiction. In the sense of being autobiography, he incorporates his personal history in the book as a rough timeline of the whole book and a basic structure
while being ready to spring up to the fictional and metaphysical level of his
art. In the sense of being a fiction, Nabokov makes use of various literary techniques to represent his self in his personal history. In the process of the representation of the self, Nabokov entangles his self with the histories of his motherland
and his foreign experiences along the journeys to various countries in his exile
life. In this sense, the personal self becomes a cultural self where different
forces of the culture unavoidably encounter with each other and makes impact on
the self. Staying in the countries where the Russian émigrés choose to stay out of
political reasons, Nabokov can only utter his speaking "I" in the marginalized
position. In such a hybrid interstice where the personal and the public, the past
and the present, the self and the other meet, Nabokov personalizes his cultural
position in artistic ways and individuates it through his life and artistic practices,

voicing the inside of the self through literary ruses that outward the inside in the other. In the journey of his lifelong exile, Nabokov never ceases to invent his self. While incorporating the foreignness of the each of the countries that he had stayed, Nabokov discovers something familiar and recurrent in the newly borrowed strangeness. During the traveling, Nabokov starts to implant his marginalized "I" in various soils and cultures while repeating in the foreign place his old self that haunts him no matter where he stays. The "I" that is resulted from this combination of the original "I" in his Russian past with the new cultural locus is always seen as a new "I", created out of the common life practices and banalities that can best represent an individual's experience of discrimination and displacement brought by the exile life. Performed through everyday practice, Nabokov's self is seen changing, evolving, and uttering its own voice out of the interstices of culture. Outwarding his personal in his depictions of his marginalized life experiences in *Speak, Memory* and transforming his home into the "beyond", Nabokov positively and creatively reverses the foreignness of the public into the familiar of the personal—his Russian past and transforms the world into his home, a Russia that is lost but regained through his art.

As an exiled writer, a witness and a victim of cultural displacement and social discrimination, Nabokov contemplates his self in this hostile situation as a positive constructing force that can perform "negating activity" as what Frantz Fanon, the Martinican psychoanalyst and participant in the Alegrian revolution says:

As soon as I *desire* I am asking to be considered. I am not merely here-and-now, sealed into thingness. I am for somewhere else and for something else. I demand that notice be taken of my negating activity insofar as I pursue something other than life; in sofar as I do battle for the creation of a human world—that is a world of reciprocal recognitions. (Bhabha 1337)

This "negating activity" is a notion that breaks the "instrumental hypothesis" (Bhabha 1337) so as to take the experience of history beyond it: "In the world in which I travel, I am endlessly creating myself. And it is by going beyond the historical, instrumental hypothesis that I will initiate my cycle of freedom" (Bhabha 1337). By negating the already existed hypothesis, Nabokov implants into the established boundaries of the nations and cultures his creative perceptions, life practices and unique understandings of the exile. Asserting a space of creations and inventions, Nabokov utters the speech of a writer who is displaced and marginalized by language, culture and politics. His speech is of the cultural hybridity, transplanting his voice of self in a foreign environment of culture. This is where something "beyond" occurs as an interstice, a possibility where creative invention can be added into existence. The "somewhere else and something else" for Fanon is where he introduces a creative element into his reconstruction of the interstices. There he hopes for going beyond the time-barrier and space limitations for a mutual recognition.

Asking for the recognition of cultural presence, Fanon establishes a boundary, a "beyond" that Bhabha calls a bridge "where 'presencing' begins because it captures something of the estranging sense of the relocation of the home and the world—the unhomeliness—that is the condition of extra-territorial and cross-cultural initiations" (Bhabha 1337). Playing with Freud's idea of unheimlich and heimlich, Bhabha introduces it into his cultural analysis. In psychological context, the unheimlich that should be repressed turns out to be the heimlich and the heimlich returns in an unheimlich way, causing the subjects an uncanny feeling. The discovery that the unfamiliar is actually from the familiar shocks the subject and he comes to recognize his repressed part of the self. In cultural context, for those diasporic writers, Bhabha believes that they strive for a "beyond", an interstice where the unhomeliness haunts them, creeping up stealthily, but familiar in its origin. Playing with the word "unheimlich" that Freud uses, Bhabha transforms it into the word unhomely, or unhomeliness that the diasporic writers experience as the condition of extra-territorial and cross-cultural initiation. Being unhomed from the motherland, the diasporic writers have for themselves a space of "beyond" to utter their lives in-between their homelands and foreign lands, merging the two in culture, language and ways of thinking. The "beyond" is also where the presencing begins. The presencing of the cultural hybridity throws the "now" afore. It is no longer the nostalgic of the homeland and the sentimentalization of the past. It is the reconstruction of the past through the addition of the present conditions, the present language, and the present culture that have unconsciously infiltrated into the mind of these writers. The homliness thus perceived and creatively constructed is transformed into the unhomeliness that now utters itself as strange, but uniquely belonging to the everyday life experiences of the writers displaced and marginalized. In this way, "the borders between home and world become confused and, uncannily, the private and the public become part of each other, forcing upon us a vision that is as divided as it is disorienting" (Bhabha 1337). In Nabokov's case, this merging of the borders between home and world, public and private produces a self, a speaking "I" that reinscribes itself in-between boundaries. By recreating and reconstructing, Nabokov incorporates the homeliness and unhomeliness, the past and art in a creative way to utter his present cultural hybridity.

What is hidden in the definitions of cultural identities is what is forgotten and neglected by the institution or instrumental hypothesis. The hidden makes the already established symmetries, balances, and black-and-white categories uncertain while the forgetting compromises at the same time the individual elements that had been marginalized and thus neglected. The affirmation of this forgetting and the hidden is where the projection of the self reinscribes itself in the condition of extra-territory and cross-culture initiation. The writers in exile like Nabokov address the changes, differences and the otherness in their works to make the hidden shown through their artistic, obscure ways of literature. The detour taken by them needs to be fully excavated to see how the culture, the public and the unhomeliness play in their works while in mingling with the personal, individual and the homeliness. In hope of voicing the insideness of their experiences of displacement and discrimination, Nabokov and his likes project their inner feelings onto the outside objects, spaces, other people and doublings to express the intricate invasions of history into their lives. According to Emmanuel Levinas, "the real world appears in the image as it were between parentheses" (Bhabha 1342). The parentheses "effects an 'externality of the inward' as the very enunciative position of the historical and narrative subject, 'introducing into the heart of subjectivity a radical and anarchical reference to the other which in fact constitutes the inwardness of the subject" (Bhabha 1342). This outwardness of the inside in the form of the other makes it possible for us to see the self of the writer in their cultural translation and cross-cultural experiences.

To assert his position and identity, Nabokov, as a diasporic Russian writer writing in English, consciously maneuvers the unhomeliness into something that can assist him to recognize more of himself, his country and his people. In *Speak*, *Memory*, he repeatedly recalls "a ghost of the present" — "that robust reality," (*SM* 77) that is his past, as "almost pathological keenness of the retrospective faculty" (*SM* 75). The past returns to his present self as an obsession of his desire for homeliness when his present self is at an unhomely space. In this way, his present self becomes an interstice where the past and the present, the homeliness and the unhomeliness intervene with each other and fight for domination. As we know, the externality of the inward can introduce a radical and anarchical reference to the other that in fact constitutes the inwardness of the subject itself. The recalling of the past now becomes externalized as a predominant theme and framework, introducing a radical reference to the other, which is the inwardness of the subject itself. Projected outward as the other, Nabokov's past becomes an important reference for him to know his inwardness, his inside. Thus the present self refers recurrently in his works to the other, his past for reference in the process of the reconstructing his true speaking "I". The unhomely context in Nabokov's exile life thus becomes the relocations of home and world in the condition of extra-territorial and cross-culture initiation, the reconstructions of the present self based on the past self and the reorganization of the homeliness of his past in the context of the unhomely present. Therefore, it is possible to say that it is the context of the "beyond", the distancing in time-space, the unhomely extra-territorial and cross-cultural locus that makes Nabokov see his unconsciously incorporated elements of homeliness and unhomeliness in a never clearer way and thus enables his reconstruction and reinteration of the speaking "I".

In analyzing Goethe's final "Note on World Literature", Bhabha introduces another line of thought into Goethe's idea of the unconscious working as the inner nature of the nations and individual man in world literature. If the " 'previously unrecognized spiritual and intellectual needs' emerges from the imposition of 'foreign' ideas, cultural representations and structures of power," (Bhabha 1339) then what will become of the more complex cultural situation? Judged from this perspective, "the study of world literature might be the study of the way in which cultures recognize themselves through their projections of 'otherness'" (Bhabha 1339). This otherness projected outward is the very insideness of the subject itself. The departure from the culture enables one to see his culture in a more detached way so as to have a clearer view of it. The sharper and truer cognition is obtained through a distancing in time and space. This is for Nabokov a much cherished property. His witness of "supreme achievement of memory, which is the masterly use it makes of innate harmonies when gathering to its fold the suspended and wandering tonalities of the past" (*SM* 170) indicates not only his concern of the fateful power of the preexistence of pattern in life but also his conscious acknowledgement of his past as the other that assists him in reconstructing his present self. As the fictional character in his autobiography, Nabokov strives to see his "I" in a clearer way by "the same faculty of impassioned commemoration, of ceaseless return, that makes me always approach that banquet table from the outside, from the depth of the park—not from the house—as if the mind, in order to go back thither, had to do so with the silent steps of a prodigal, faint with excitement" (*SM* 171). The mind that returns is a mind that thinks in ration and in a detached distance while not excluding the pleasures and excitement brought by the artistic reconstruction and reorganization of the self.

In chapter five of *Speak*, *Memory*, Nabokov presents his memory of his most unforgettable French governess—Mademoiselle who worked is his Russian home and later returned to her home in Switzerland. Mademoiselle who stayed at his home for seven years was bitter in other people's treatment of herself and was sensitive in any remarks that might lead her to take as contempt to her and to her country. Feeling unhappy and ill-treated by the fellow staff working in Nabokov's house, Mademoiselle wrote a letter to Nabokov's mother and went back to her country. But when Nabokov years later traveled to Switzerland and paid her a visit, he is surprised to find that Mademoiselle was extremely yearning for the years she had spent in Russia and treasure her life there as the most unforgettable experience in her life. In addition, Mademoiselle is now the bosom friend of Mlle Golay who was not on speaking terms with her when they both worked in Nabokov's home in Russia. The memories shared by the two governesses in Russia make their relationship specially intimate and happy. At this, Nabokov says: "One is always at home in one's past, which partly explains those pathetic ladies' posthumous love for a remote and, to be perfectly frank, rather appalling country, which they never had really known and in which none of them had been content" (*SM* 116). This is also true to Nabokov's life. His past memories in Russia now return to him as the other—the outwardness of the inner-side of his self. This allows him to recognize that home and the self at that home in a more lucid way. Nabokov the child only caught some glimpses of his Mademoiselle— "her chins or her ways or even her French" (*SM* 117) when he was in Russia. But when he went to visit his governess in Switzerland more than a dozen of years later, he came to recognize something that he had never given thought to. His governess's deceit used to have him "depart pleased with my own kindness, or to that swan whose agony was so much closer to artistic truth than a drooping dancer's pale arms; something, in short, that I could appreciate only after the things and beings that I had most loved in the security of my childhood had been turned to ashes or shot through the heart" (*SM* 117). The homeliness, when is recognized in an unhomely context, gives one a creeping uncanny feeling and makes one realize better one's inner-side of the self.

In chapter six, the chapter of the butterflies and moths, Nabokov assigns multi-layered meanings to his life hobby. Butterfly not only reminds him of his intimate moments shared with his father but also suggests the rebirth of the dead in a new way. This metaphoric meaning of the latter is exploited by Nabokov in many of his works to hint at the rebirth of the dead body and the transformation from the physical to the spiritual. In addition to the otherworld suggestion of the butterfly, it connects Nabokov in various stages of his life and in different places of his exile life. Bringing this hobby wherever he went, Nabokov transforms butterfly and butterfly-catching into something that bridges his homeliness and his unhomeliness. In repeating the same thing—butterfly-catching in various stages of life and in various state of mind and in various countries in the journey of exile, Nabokov never ceases to pursue what butterfly has brought to his life, his art and his understanding of the world. Treating and studying butterfly in a minute and professional way both in his scientific and artistic works, Nabokov transforms it into a mobile diaspora like himself, disseminating the seeds of the flowers from one place to another. Transporting the pollen from one location to another, butterfly enlivens the fixed and static things and infuses into it the foreign elements. In the process of this dissemination, the fixed pollen with the help of butterfly becomes alive and flowing and comes to continue its existence in different environments. Likewise, Nabokov, bringing the cultural seeds of Russia and his Russian past into various places he had been, acts the same role in transplanting the home in an international context. The result of it is the introduction of the new and foreign elements into Russian culture, gaining for Russian culture more dimensions and perspectives in judging both national and international cultural affairs. At the same time, Nabokov's recalling of his home culture is extended from its original narrow sense and is enlarged into the international context where new and foreign elements make the original home culture stand out from the mass and makes it easier for the subject to rethink the insideness of his home culture that has been taken for granted in the unconscious way.

A very keen example of Nabokov's conscious exploration of his self, his Russian past and his home culture is illustrated in chapter five of *Speak*, *Memory*. Here during the readings of Mademoiselle on the veranda where Nabokov can look at the garden below through the harlequin pattern of colored panes inset in a whitewashed framework on either side of the veranda:

The garden when viewed through these magic glasses grew strangely still and aloof. If one looked through blue glass, the sand turned to cinders while inky trees swam in a tropical sky. The yellow creates an amber world infused with an extra strong brew of sunshine. The red made the foliage drip ruby dark upon a pink footpath. The green soaked greenery in a greener green. And when, after such richness, one turned to a small square of normal, savorless glass, with its lone mosquito or lame daddy longlegs, it was like taking a draught of water when one is not thirsty, and one saw a matter-of – fact white bench under familiar trees. But of all the windows this is the pane through which in later years parched nostalgia longed to peer. (*SM* 106—107)

The objects in the garden looked through the magic glass lose their common, ordinary and taken-for-granted reality and are tinged with an aloofness and stillness. The familiar things looked through a "normal, savorless glass" have been unconsciously accepted by the normal minds and thus turned into part of the everyday life reality. Reduced to things that are transparent in our lives, the objects in Nabokov's Russian villa garden lose their enigmatic charm and glamour. When the same things are filtered through the magic glass of colors, the plain and flat scenery is transformed into a remote land of beauty. Through different colors of glass of memory and imagination of a subject who is deeply soaked in various foreign territories and cross-cultural contexts, the homeliness of the past are hence transplanted into an unhomely moment through the creative transformations and artistic reconstructions of the present self.

The colored glass that transforms Nabokov's views refers to both his imaginative/artistic reconstruction and his international context. The former distances and defamiliarizes the artist in time and space while the latter lends Nabokov a consciousness to capture the beauty of his home culture that has been taken for granted as something trivial and useless. Thus the homeliness and unhomeliness combined when the unhomeliness is recognized through the recalling of the homeliness. In this way, the bland scenery that has been unconsciously accepted as a commonality is hence re-cognized and re-presented as almost different scenery with only some shadows of the original fragments left in this enchanting glamour of the alien atmosphere in the magic view. The new view thus produced contains the interactions of homeliness and the unhomeliness, the past and the present, the home and the world. These pairs are no longer set in fixed boundaries, but merge with each other in this process of cultural translation and cultural hybidity. A true cultural hybidity is thus better seen in these comparisons of different cultures and a truer self is thus captured by a calm and rational mind which belongs to a modern writer with romantic emotions.

Nabokov's return to the past in both physical and spiritual sense is in retrospective viewed by him as his conscious return and at the same time an inherent trait from his parents. Both as a latterly constructed performative act and an unconscious fate in his life, the return, after the first conscious return in a physical sense at the age of not quite six, only takes place in his imagination: after being abroad for a year,

> against the background of winter, the ceremonial change of cars and engines acquired a strange new meaning···that particular return to Russia, my first *conscious* return, seems to me now, sixty years later, a rehearsal—not of the grand homecoming that will never take place, but of its constant dream in my long years of exile. (*SM* 96—97)

The never-happened return after his early age is transformed into an artistic traveling for home, for his Russian past. This traveling in mind and imagination in both his life and works can function as the physical return that brings him "a strange new meaning" to his culture, his mother tongue and his self in that land. His love of his country and his nostalgic obsession transplant Russia in the places he went on exile and "give me anything on any continent resembling the St. Petersburg countryside and my heart melts" (*SM* 250). This active reconstruction of his Russian past in any places that may remind him of it is obviously Nabokov's individual tact or art that turns the foreign, marginalized and discriminated situations into his battle ground where he creatively voices his position as a diasporic writer.

As what has been said by Bhabha, "as literary creatures and political animals we ought to concern ourselves with the understanding of human action and the social world as a moment when "something is beyond control, but it is not

beyond accommodation" (Bhabha 1340). That means writers of exile can take
the advantage of their marginalized position in a subversive way so as to explore
in a cross-cultural way the living practice and rituals which introduce richness
formerly hidden below the instrumental hypothesis. For Bhabha, this act of writing the world, taking the measure of its dwelling is captured by Morrison in her
house of fiction, art as "the fully realized presence of a haunting of history"
(Bhabha 1340). Nabokov is also holding this intention in his art, only in a
more deceptive way. For Nabokov, art itself is his ultimate aim; the pursuit of
the otherworld is aimed for the ecstasy and happiness that are created out of his
art. But one can not fail to detect his concern for his émigré status, his lifelong
exile, his resulted fate from the external world affairs and the poignancy of losing his beloved family members and friends. Giving greatest concern to the status
of the Russian émigré writers in Berlin and Paris, Nabokov artistically transforms these cultural elements into the material of his art by giving his characters
the traits of his and his fellow émigré writers. Therefore, lying underneath his
art, a concern to his past and present cultural contexts can always be detected
in the "parentheses" where the truth is kept. Mentioned in a passing way, his
concern and his judgment on his cultural hybidity, cultural displacement and
discrimination should not be neglected. Rather, it provides us a view of the diasporic writers' reality.

Transforming politics "from a pedagogical, ideological practice to politics
as a performativity," (Bhabha 1341) Nabokov introduces us to his unhomely
house of everyday practice where the poignancy of the diasporas is best represented. His loneliness and bleakness could well be imagined in a foreign country
where "no real communication, of the rich human sort so widespread in our own
midst, existed between us and them" (SM 276). But Nabokov is actively turning it into a "beyond" where he and other émigré writers gain their spiritual independence in their intense cultural atmosphere "with a coefficient of culture
that greatly surpassed the cultural mean of the necessarily more diluted foreign
communities among which they were placed" (SM 277). Standing out in a never
stronger assertion in literary circle, Nabokov is also conscious of his fellow
émigrés who make the fool of the institutions in maneuvering their own life in a

creative way: "Sweet are the recollections some Russian émigrés treasure of how they insulted or fooled high officials at various ministries···" (*SM* 277) Admiring these "ways of operating" (Certeau, *The Practice of Everyday Life* xiv) in their actual reappropriation of the disciplines of the institutions, Nabokov and his fellow émigrés creatively transform their everyday practice into an ingenious battle ground to subvert the oppressions imposed on them. Along with their artistic creation, the past and present life of Nabokov and his Russian émigrés as presented in their works best voices a speaking self that reinscribes itself in-between artistic recreation and ghostly past.

Conclusion

The three books that I have chosen to discuss in my book pinpoint the three aspects of viewing Nabokov's art and life though the three books share the same artistic characters that reign in all of Nabokov's art. As his early Russian novel, *Invitation to a Beheading* depicts a character called Cincinnatus who is put into prison of time and space of this world simply out of his difference from all the other people. By cornering Cincinnatus into an isolated situation that everyone in the mundane world shows contempt and casts doubts, Nabokov tests the spiritual pursuit of the otherworld carried by Cincinnatus in the mundane world context. Confronting the hostile feelings and threatening from all aspects of the society—the family, the neighbors, the school teachers and classmates, the lover, the government, Cincinnatus is pressed to his own spiritual and imaginative world where, when he is observed and monitored, his double enters for the timelessness, bliss and happiness that the mundane world can never offer. Cincinnatus's split life—the life in the mundane world and life in his otherworld at first is bearable since he can at least escape the stuffy and cruel society of the mundane into his ecstasy of Tamara Gardens that houses his most cherished memories. At the same time, he has illusion with his lover whom he believes will finally have faith in him and his ideas.

However, through a series of episodes which take place during the time of his imprisonment, his trusted ones disappoint him one after another. His fellow cell friend who he believes is trying to save him turned out to be the executioner who carries with him a mission of convincing Cincinnatus of his satisfaction with the death sentence that the government had made. The child of the director of the prison whom Cincinnatus thought might have a soft and pure heart hints at a rescue turns out to play a mischievous joke with him so that she has something to write about. After finally seeing that his lover/wife is beyond the hope of sharing with him his cherished romantic feelings that they have had in the Tarmara Gardens, Cincinnatus is eventually capable of standing on his own to strive for the otherworld dream by sacrificing his physical body that houses his spiritual one. The course of gradually keeping aloof from the heartless and cruel mundane space and freeing from the mundane world sets a dramatic and fantastic atmosphere for the two spaces—the mundane and the otherworld. In transcending the mundane into the space of the otherworld, Cincinnatus gains his full-sense spiritual freedom, abandoning the mundane world where people live an unimaginative and dead life. Obtaining another perspective of looking at this world, Nabokov, in this fantasy novel, shows us a space of the otherworld where the self, through itself and its double/other's moving back and forth between the two spaces, inserts its voice and gains a metaphysical understanding of the self.

In *The Real Life of Sebastian Knight*, Nabokov self-consciously creates a literary world with great intricacy, complicating the boundaries between the real/verisimilitude and the "real". The narrator-cum-biographer V. creates a personal history of his half-brother Sebastian Knight who is both a writer and a biographee in his biography. The reliability of the narration of V. is constantly put into question because of his own subjective construction and his gradual inclination toward and instinctive obsession with his dead half-brother's spirit. V. , gradually being absorbed by the life and art of Sebastian, comes to recognization that his book about the real life of his half-brother can never be real enough according to the commonsense standard. The only real thing is the fictionality itself that has all the way been unconsciously invented and created by both himself and his Sebastian Knight. The book creates a fictional framework that embeds another fictional world of biography in which characters are both existed in the same ontological level with the narrator and in another ontological level different from the narrator. In the process of writing of the biography, V. is gaining more and more insights from his study of Sebastian's life, work, art and spirit. He, at the end of the book, is so absorbed into the work he is undertaking that he says that Sebastian Knight is I and I am Sebastian Knight.

Traveling back and forth between his real world of businesses and

Sebastian's world of the otherworld art, V. gradually loses his ration and commonsense that all the people of the real world cherish and tends to be guided by the spirit of the late Sebastian Knight so as to write the preexistent "real" life of Sebastian Knight. In this intricate aesthetic world of art, Sebastian and the V. at the end of the book are all pursuing the otherworld sensibility. Both desire it: Sebastian is following his blood in composing his works, the blood that has inherited his dead mother's capriciousness and uncertainty. His love of a dark lady facilitates him to finally reach his otherworld in art and life though this love affair in a way leads him to his final doom. V. , in taking the mission of writing a life story of his half-brother, gradually follows the guidance of his late brother and composes a work that is actually written in a spiritual and insubstantial way by the dead Sebastian. As a character, Sebastian Knight lives, writes and makes friends male and female to feel the rhythm of life, the life of the past spent in Russia and the life in various countries in Europe. During this process, his inherent love for freedom in life and art comes to possess him and he comes to express it both in life and art. In his artistic works, he is seen gradually abandoning his mundane touch with the reality and seeks for something that is connected with the timeless space of the otherworld. Deeply steeped in his artistic pursuit and greatly delighted in the bliss brought by his art, Sebastian comes to be near his final aim of life after the composition of his last novel.

As a narrator, V. collects the materials left by any possible sources by Sebastian and creatively reconstructs them in his own way. During his journey and interviews for the purpose of collecting the real facts of Sebastian's life, he seems to see Sebastian's artistic works as more fascinating than the physical, matter-of-fact life of Sebastian. Step by step, V. is deeply involved in the literary works and delightful atmospheres that Sebastian has represented in his works. He even comes to comment and expand the works of Sebastian. Along with his efforts for the real facts of Sebastian, V. obtains, through his devotion to the spirit of the dead Sebastian, the "real" that is his own subjective interpretation of the real facts collected in the process. The "real" that is nearer to Sebastian's spiritual pursuit transports V into someone that almost shares Nabokov's ideas and sentiments. V. 's pursuit of the "real" life of Sebastian

Knight serves as an important literary ruse for Nabokov to distance himself from his fictional characters and at the same time also transports himself to the space of the otherworld to explore his self between the real facts of the verisimilitude of the traditional novels and the "real" /the imaginative. Moving back and forth between the real/reality and the "real" /imaginative, Nabokov inserts his voice in this literary context his speaking "I" through the doubling of his character/narrator into a fictional writer—Sebastian. Thus, Nabokov gains an artistic way of expressing his literary ideas and concerns through creating fictional spaces where the otherworld sensibility is intricately delivered out while the speaking "I" asserts his position in this aesthetic enigma.

In *Speak, Memory*, Nabokov the writer and Nabokov the character/narrator merge into each other when he declares that this autobiography is designed between the genre of fiction and the genre of autobiography. Consciously recalling his past memories, Nabokov fuses his artistic strategies with his fragments of his past. Therefore, those seemingly unrelated life episodes are constructed as connecting with each other in a fateful way and the pattern thus formulated serves as an essence of the autobiography to coalesce the pearls of the memories into a meaningful and epiphanic watermark that overrules the whole work. This conscious construction of one's past is closely connected with Nabokov's experience of the exile. Being marginalized and displaced from his home culture, Nabokov in his journeys of exile refuses to fix his self as a static identity, but as a flowing and changing position in his consistently comparing of his Russian culture with the culture of the other nations. In this constant movement from one culture to another, Nabokov distances himself from his home culture in time and space only to see his home culture in a clearer and conscious way.

The already taken-for-granted culture of Russia is renovatively expressed through Nabokov's literary imagination, rational thinking, objective analysis and profound emotional longings. This thus introduces a new voice of marginalized people as Nabokov the diasporic writer into the already fixed categories of cultural identities. Nabokov in *Speak, Memory* locates himself in an extra-territorial and cross-cultural initiation where his past that should be repressed returns as something familiar in his present time and space. As a result of this, the homeliness and the unhomeliness are combined to form his new understanding of his self. Moving from past and present, art and the memory, the speaking "I" in *Speak*, *Memory* unceasingly reconstructs the returned past. The returned past in an international context appears to obtain a new meaning in that the reflection of the past in the present framework takes on an exceptionally clear image. With the consciousness of explaining the present "I" through the past "I" and elucidating the past "I" at a distance both in time and space, Nabokov joins his past "I" and his present "I" creatively in the process of self-exploration in order that the two can inter-elucidate each other. Therefore, under the textual space of the otherworld which transforms the writer into another timeless consciousness, the speaking "I", in moving between art and memory, past and present, homeliness and unhomeliness, reinscribes itself by artistically recognizing the returned past in his unconscious in a conscious way.

With the discussion of the three major novels in Nabokov's mature period of writing, the book opens a way to approach Nabokov from three complementary perspectives—metaphysical, literary and cultural. The three approaches are discussed in the context of Nabokov's otherworld concern that underscores every one of his works. In the light of otherworld, Nabokov strives for the impossible, that is, breaking the time sphere or prison of this world and obtaining a timeless consciousness that enables one to enjoy the artistic ecstasy of the otherworld. In this context, Nabokov expresses himself in many ways to regain his lost Russian past that obsesses him for his lifelong time and creates the other to outward his innermost sentiments and emotions. For further research, we can further explore the otherness as related with the speaking "I" in many other novels of Nabokov to see how he speaks through masks and literary disguises of his characters and images in the textual space so as to relieve him of his desire of Russian past. In addition, Nabokov, through historical, cultural and social contexts that seem to be pushed to the marginal place in his fictional works, makes clear his position among various forces of the external reality. It is through his profusion of art that his cultural position is more profoundly uttered. Therefore, the way Nabokov's art weaves cultural elements deserves our attention. Through putting Nabokov's art in an enlarged context, we can see how Nabokov, through his unique art, responds to the outside society. In addition, the concrete ways of his other as a doubling of himself in addressing and acknowledging the culture should also be explored so that we can see how his claim of making the readers behave in a conscious and creative way in many issues of cultural importance can be a call for a more humane and better society.

Bibliography

Primary Works:

Nabokov, Vladimir,

——, *Conclusive Evidence: A Memoir*, New York: Harper, 1951.

——, *The Gift*, Middlesex: Penguin, 1983.

——, *Invitation to a Beheading*, Middlesex: Penguin, 1983.

——, *Lectures on Literature*, New York: Harcourt Brace Jovanovich, 1980.

——, *Lectures on Russian Literature*, ed. Fredson Bowers, New York: Harcourt Brace Jovanovich/Bruccoli, 1981.

——, *Mary*, Middlesex: Penguin Book, 1971.

——, *Nikolai Gogol*, New York: New Directions, 1961.

——, *The Real Life of Sebastian Knight*, Norfolk, New York: New Directions, 1941.

——, *Selected Letters*, San Diego: Harcourt Brace Jovanovich, 1968.

——, *The Stories of Vladimir Nabokov*, Middlesex: Penguin, 1995.

——, *Speak, Memory*, New York: G. P. Putnam's Sons, 1966.

——, *Strong Opinions*, New York: McGraw-Hill, 1973.

Secondary Works:

Alexandrov, Vladimir E. , *Nabokov's Otherworld*, New Jersey: Princeton University Press, 1991.

——, *The Garland Companion to Vladimir Nabokov*, New York & London: Garland Publishing INC. , 1995.

Andrews, David, *Aestheticism, Nabokov, and Lolita*, Vol.. 31, New

York: The Edwin Mellen Press, 1999.

Appel, Alfred Jr. , *Nabokov: Criticism, Reminiscences, Translations and Tributes*, Eds. London: Weidenfeld and Nicolson, 1970.

Bachelard, Gaston, *The Poetics of Space*, New York: The Orion Press, 1964.

Bader, Julia, *Crystal land: Artifice in Nabokov's English Novels*, Oakland: University of California Press, 1972.

Bethea, David M. , "Style", *The Garland Companion to Vladimir Nabokov*, Ed. Vladimir E. Alexandrov, New York & London: Garland Publishing INC. , 1995.

Bhabha, Homi K. , "Locations of Culture", *The Critical Tradition: Classical Texts and Contemporary Trends*, ed. David H Richter, New York: Bedford/St. Martin's, 1998.

——, *Location of Culture*, Routledge, 1994.

Blackwell, Stephen, *The Quill and the Scalpel*, Ohio: The Ohio State University, 2009.

Bloom, Harold, *Vladimir Nabokov's Lolita*, Ed. New York: Chelsea House Publishers, 1987.

——, *Modern Critical Views: Vladimir Nabokov*. Ed. New York: Chelsea House Publishers. 1987.

Boyd, Brian, *Nabokov's Ada*, New Zealand: Cybereditions Cooperation, 2001.

——, *Vladimir Nabokov: The Russian Years*, New Jersey: Princeton UP, 1990.

——, *Vladimir Nabokov: The American Years*, New Jersey: Princeton UP, 1991.

——, *Nabokov's Pale Fire*, New Jersey: Princeton UP, 1999.

Clancy, Laurie, *The Novels of Vladimir Nabokov*, Macmillan, 1984.

Clegg, Christine, *Lolita: A Reader's Guide to Essential Criticism*, London: Icon Books, 2000.

Certeau, de Michel, *Heterologies: Discourse on the Other*, trans. Brian Massumi, Minnesoda: University of Minnesoda Press, 1988.

——, *Culture in the Plural*, Minneapolis: University of Minnesota Press, 1974.

——, *The Practice of Everyday Life*, trans. Steven Rendall, California: University of California Press, 1988.

——, *The Writing of History*, New York: Columbia University Press, 1988.

Connolly, Julian W., *Nabokov's Early Fiction: Patterns of Self and Other*, Cambridge: Cambridge University Press, 1992.

——, *Nabokov's "Invitation to a Beheading"*, Ed. Illinois: Northwestern UP., 1997.

Cornwell, Neil, *Vladimir Nabokov*, Tavistock: Northcote House Publisher Ltd., 1999.

——, *Nabokov and His Fiction: New Perspectives*, Cambridge University Press, 1999.

Dembo. L. S., *Nabokov: The Man and His Work*, Madison: The University of Wisconsin Press, 1967.

Durantaye, Leland De la, *Style and Matter: the Moral Art of Vladimir Nabokov*, Ithaca: Cornell University Press, 2007.

Diment, Galya. "Nabokov's Biographical Impulse: Art of Writing Lives", *The Cambridge Companion to Nabokov*, ed. Julian W. Connolly, Cambridge: Cambridge UP., 2005.

——, *Pniniad*, University of Washington Press, 1997.

Field, Andrew, *The Life and Art of Vladimir Nabokov*, New York: Crown Publishers Inc., 1977.

——, *Nabokov: His Life in Part*, New York: The Viking Press, 1977.

Foster, John Burt. *Nabokov's Art of Memory and European Modernism*, New Jersey: Princeton University Press, 1993.

Fowler, Douglas, *Reading Nabokov*, Intahca: Cornell University Press, 1974.

Freud, Sigmund, *The Uncanny*, Trans. David Maclintock, Middlesex: Penguin, 2003.

Grabes, H. *Fictitious Biographies: Vladimir Nabokov's English Novels*,

The Hague: Mouton publishers, 1977.

Grayson, Jane and Arnold Mcmillin *Nabokov's World*, eds. Vol. 1, New York: Palgrave, 2002.

——, *Nabokov's World*, eds. Vol. 2. New York: Palgrave, 2002.

Green, Geoffery, *Freud and Nabokov*, Lincoln: University of Nebraska Press, 1988.

Johnson, Kurt and Steve Coates, *Nabokov's Blues*, Hanover: Zoland Books, 1999.

Khrushcheva, Nina L. , *Imagining Nabokov*, New Haven: Yale University Press, 2007.

Hyde, G. M. , *Vladimir Nabokov: America's Russian Novelist*, London: Marion Boyars, 1974.

Larmour, David H. J. , ed. *Discourse and Ideology in Nabokov's Prose*, Routledge, 2002.

Lee, L. L. , *Vladimir Nabokov*, Boston: Twayne Publishers, 1976.

Long, Michael, *Marvell, Nabokov: Childhood and Arcadia*, Oxford: Clarendon Press, 1984.

Maddox, Lucy, *Nabokov's Novels in English*, Athens: The University of Georgia Press, 1983.

McHale, Brian, *Postmodernist Fiction*, London: Methuen, 1987.

Norman, Will, *Transitional Nabokov*, Eds. New York: Peter Lang, 2008.

Page, Norman, *Nabokov: The Critical Heritage*, Routledge, 1982.

Packman, David, *Vladimir Nabokov: The Structure of Literary Desire*, Columbia: University of Missouri Press, 1982.

Parker, Stephen Jan. , *Understanding Vladimir Nabokov*, Columbia: University of South Carolina Press, 1987.

Piffer, Ellen, *Nabokov and the Novel*, Boston: Harvard University Press, 1980.

Quennell, Peter, *Vladimir Nabokov: A Tribute*, New York: William Morrow and Company INC. , 1980.

Rampton, David, *Vladimir Nabokov*, Macmillan, 1993.

Rivkin, Julie & Michael Ryan, *Literary Theory: An Anthology*, Blackwell, 2004.

Rorty, Richard, *Contingency, Irony, and Solidarity*, Cambridge: Cambridge University Press, 1989.

Roth, Phyllis A., *Critical Essays on Vladimir Nabokov*, Boston: G. K. Hall & Co., 1984.

Rowe, William Woodin, *Nabokov's Deceptive World*, New York: New York UP., 1971.

——, *Nabokov's Spectral Dimension*, Ardis: Ann Arbor, 1981.

Sharpe, Tony, *Vladimir Nabokov*, Lancaster University press, 1991.

Shrayer, Maxim, *The World of Nabokov's Stories*, Austin: University of Texas Press, 1999.

Sisson, J. B., "The Real Life of Sebastian Life", *The Garland Companion to Vladimir Nabokov*, Ed. Vladimir Alexandrov, New York & London: Garland Publishing INC., 1995.

Soja, W., *Thirdspace*, Blackwell, 1996.

Stegner, Page, *The Art of Vladimir Nabokov: Escape into Aesthetics*, New York: The Dial Press, 1966.

Stuart, Dabney, *Nabokov: The Dimensions of Parody*, Los Angeles: Louisiana State University Press, 1978.

Thacker, Andrew, *Moving Through Modernity*, Manchester & New York: Manchester University Press, 2003.

Wood, Michael, *The Magician's Doubts*, London: Chatto & Windus, 1994.

Zunshine, Lisa, *Nabokov at the Limits*, Ed. New York: Garland Publishing Inc, 1999.

何岳球:《〈洛丽塔〉: 纳博科夫的"变态"蝴蝶》,《外国文学研究》2008 年第 5 期。

——:《纳博科夫的蝴蝶情节和美学意蕴》,《当代外国文学》2007 年第 1 期。

黄铁池:《玻璃彩球中的蝶线: 纳博科夫及其〈洛丽塔〉解读》,《外国文学评论》2002 年第 2 期。

赵君:《探寻现实的"本真"内涵:论纳博科夫"后现代式"的现实观》,《外国文学评论》2008 年第 4 期。

周启超:《独特的文化身份与"独特的彩色纹理"——双语作家纳博科夫文学世界的跨文化特征》,《外国文学评论》2003 年第 4 期。